Kent's arms encircled her bare waist to steady her on the gently rocking raft, and Morgan trembled despite the warmth of the sun.

"Cold?" he murmured.

"No," she said too quickly.

"Does this feel better?" he asked, stroking her shoulders.

"No," she whispered huskily.

"No?" he challenged, his hands moving up her throat to cup her chin. He studied her face, seeming to read her distrust . . . and desire. Then slowly, lazily, his face descended until his lips touched hers as gently as a flower petal, tasting, savoring their cool velvet wetness.

RUTH LANGAN
describes herself as a full time mother and part time writer. Happily married to her childhood sweetheart, her busy household includes five beautiful children. Tiny and blond, she skis, bowls, golfs and jogs several miles each day.

Dear Reader:

Silhouette has always tried to give you exactly what you want. When you asked for increased realism, deeper characterization and greater length, we brought you Silhouette Special Editions. When you asked for increased sensuality, we brought you Silhouette Desire. Now you ask for books with the length and depth of Special Editions, the sensuality of Desire, but with something else besides, something that no one else offers. Now we bring you SILHOUETTE INTIMATE MOMENTS, true romance novels, longer than the usual, with all the depth that length requires. More sensuous than the usual, with characters whose maturity matches that sensuality. Books with the ingredient no one else has tapped: excitement.

There is an electricity between two people in love that makes everything they do magic, larger than life—and this is what we bring you in SILHOUETTE INTIMATE MOMENTS. Look for them this May, wherever you buy books.

These books are for the woman who wants more than she has ever had before. These books are for you. As always, we look forward to your comments and suggestions. You can write to me at the address below:

Karen Solem
Editor-in-Chief
Silhouette Books
P.O. Box 769
New York, N.Y. 10019

RUTH LANGAN
Hidden Isle

Silhouette Romance

Published by Silhouette Books New York

America's Publisher of Contemporary Romance

Other Silhouette Books by Ruth Langan

Just Like Yesterday

 SILHOUETTE BOOKS, a Simon & Schuster Division of
GULF & WESTERN CORPORATION
1230 Avenue of the Americas, New York, N.Y. 10020

ISBN: 0-671-57224-5

First Silhouette Books printing May, 1983

10 9 8 7 6 5 4 3 2 1

Map by Ray Lundgren

To Tom, who always believed.

Hidden
Isle

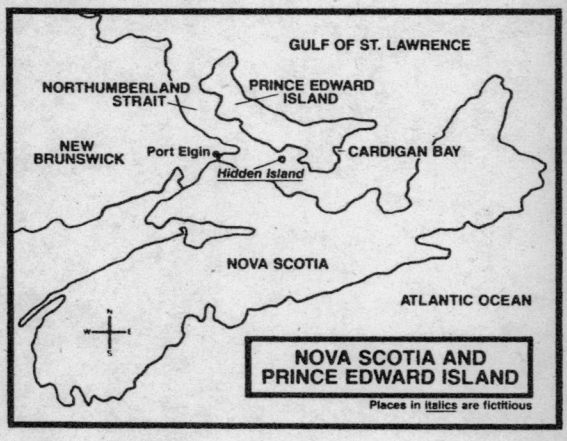

GULF OF ST. LAWRENCE

NORTHUMBERLAND
STRAIT

PRINCE EDWARD
ISLAND

NEW
BRUNSWICK

Port Elgin

Hidden Island

CARDIGAN BAY

NOVA SCOTIA

ATLANTIC OCEAN

N
W—E
S

**NOVA SCOTIA AND
PRINCE EDWARD ISLAND**

Places in *italics* are fictitious

Chapter One

Morgan Anders peered through the rain-streaked windows of the car. There was nothing to see but eerie darkness punctuated by flashes of lightning. She tried the key in the ignition once more. Nothing. The battery must be dead. In frustration she leaned her head back and let out an angry sigh. What to do now? She huddled in the darkened car and pondered her dismal situation.

She knew it was her own fault for being in this predicament. Nearly two hours ago she had driven through a fairly large town. She should have stopped at a motel for the night and completed her journey refreshed in the morning. The strain of the six-hundred-mile drive from New York to the quiet beauty of New Brunswick, in Canada, was taking its toll. Before the darkness of the stormy night had closed in, Morgan had thrilled to the primitive beauty along the route. The highway, winding along majestic cliffs beside the Saint Lawrence Seaway, offered glimpses of the savage beauty of the Maritime Provinces of Canada. She had forgotten her stiff muscles as she drove past magnificent red cliffs and tunneled rocks, or slowly passed through postcard-perfect little towns, with their brilliantly painted houses of red, orange, pink and green. Each yard sprouted a string of fresh, white laundry billowing on the breeze, as if in celebration of the summer sun. Every village had a church with tall spires and pealing bells, a grassy park or village green with its latticework gazebo and the Quebec flag, the Fleur-de-Lis, flying from its tall flagpole.

The teeming city streets, with their colorful throngs of office workers on noonday breaks; the street-corner vendors hawking their wares; the honking horns of irate cabdrivers; the heat of the city seeming to rise up from the very pavement—all these images seemed to fade away as the small car threaded its way through quiet towns and curving ribbons of highway. But now, with the storm-darkened night angrily blotting all other scenes from view, the quaint villages and their warm welcome were forgotten. As usual, Morgan realized that it was her impulsive nature that had gotten her into trouble.

She switched on a flashlight and studied the map. According to the sign she had passed a short time ago, she must be within walking distance of Port Elgin, the town in New Brunswick where she would board a ferry for Hidden Island, her final destination. Should she try to walk, or sit here and hope that a car would stop? With sinking heart she realized that she hadn't seen another vehicle for at least half an hour. And the longer she sat here, the later it got. Morgan glanced down at her sandals and the delicate silk dress that clung to her soft curves. The eager salesgirl in New York had cleverly sold her on the expensive outfit, assuring her that the deep rose color was a perfect contrast to her thick, dark hair and expressive brown eyes and that it would put a bloom on her cheeks. After catching Morgan's attention with all that flattery, the sale had been easy. Morgan splurged on these clothes so she could make a good impression on her new employer. She frowned now at her silly extravagance. She wouldn't be able to walk a block in these shoes. And silk dresses weren't made for cold, stormy nights. Leaning over the seat, she rummaged through her suitcase for something practical. In a few minutes she had removed the dress and had pulled on a flannel shirt and jeans and had replaced the sandals with canvas sneakers. She hadn't packed a raincoat. A cotton poplin jacket wouldn't offer much protection in this downpour, but it would have to do.

Morgan knew the luggage would have to be left behind in the car. It was too heavy to carry. Into a small overnight case she stuffed her essentials: her purse, a change of underthings, a pair of cotton shorts and a shirt. For a few more minutes she studied the road map, then, mentally marking the route she would follow, she stuffed the map and the flashlight into her overnight bag. With a careful glance around the car, she locked the door, dropped the keys into the bag, and walked slowly into the storm-blackened night.

Within minutes her long, silken strands of black hair were plastered against her neck and face. Her thick, dark eyelashes blinked against the torrent. The rain-soaked jeans clung to her legs as she walked. The jacket and flannel shirt stuck like a sodden clump against her clammy skin.

At a fork in the road Morgan studied the signs, then turned left. Two miles to Port Elgin, she told herself. Two miles. She jumped at a sudden crash of thunder and stepped, unseeing, into a black puddle. Her shoes made a squishing sound with every step. The handle of the overnight bag dug into her palm. Oh, why had she gotten herself into this predicament? What had ever possessed her to leave her familiar surroundings in the city for this desolate place in Canada? Morgan's grim mouth tightened. Her thoughts were as bleak as the landscape. The answer was simple. Money, of course. Enough money to replace that rickety car back there on the road. With no family to turn to since the death of her grandfather last year, twenty-year-old Morgan Anders had to make it on her own. As she thought of Gramps, her tears mingled with the rain that streamed down her cheeks.

Poor Gramps. He thought he had taken care of everything before his death. The little handwritten slip of paper leaving his meager belongings and frugal bank account to his only granddaughter had been carefully placed in a sealed envelope with instructions for it to be opened only after his death.

Morgan had spent a lifetime with her grandfather and never once had heard him mention a brother. But after the death notice in the paper, a man had shown up at Morgan's door with proof that he was indeed a brother and, according to a legally documented will, had been left everything. The paper had been dated nearly forty years earlier, when both her grandfather and his brother were younger men. Apparently they had both signed the will, leaving all to either survivor.

When Morgan checked with a legal advisor, she was given the sad news that the stranger's copy of the will was legal and had been witnessed and dated. The handwritten paper entrusted to Morgan's care had not been witnessed. The lawyer advised her that there was nothing she could do to change the fact that this stranger had a legitimate claim. His background had been thoroughly checked. He was her grandfather's brother. So, Morgan conceded her loss.

During this last year Morgan had learned not to dwell on the past but to look forward instead to the future. After all, she was young, healthy, bright and willing to work hard for what she wanted. And Gramps had left her a legacy after all—the legacy of a curious, seeking mind, a determined self-reliance, an impish sense of humor and a zest for life. These were the things money couldn't buy, possessions no one could ever take from her.

In April, Morgan had been forced to ride the bus

to work while her car was in repair. Someone had left a folded newspaper on a seat. To pass the time, Morgan had absently picked it up. The words of the ad nearly leaped off the page at her. It read: "Capable secretary, willing to spend summer at Canadian lodge on secluded island. Must have excellent references." The salary listed was good, far better than the money Morgan earned at Fairfield Academy, an exclusive boys' school, where she worked in the office during the school year while completing her college education at night. It was nearly double what she was paid as assistant counselor at a summer camp in upstate New York where she had worked in past summers. The higher salary would enable her to buy the new car she knew she would have to have within the year.

Morgan had torn out the small ad and stuffed it into her purse. Later, at the office, she had typed her application and mailed it to the post office box listed in the ad. A month later she had received the letter indicating that the job was hers. A map had been enclosed showing the route to Hidden Island. She had rejoiced at this unexpected opportunity for summer employment.

Morgan shivered in the driving wind and rain. As she trudged up the dirt road, she spotted lights in the distance. Port Elgin. She smiled despite her misery. She had made it through two miles of darkened, rutted, rain-soaked roads. Shifting the bag to her other hand, she quickened her pace.

At a small grocery store she peered through dirt-smudged windows. Although lights burned within, the store was closed for the night. She trudged further along the main street and stopped at a gas station.

"Hello, miss. Bad night to be walking." The accent was decidedly French.

Morgan stared at the old man in the doorway. Her large, brown eyes widened in happiness. She was so relieved to see another human being, she could have hugged him.

"Oh. Thank goodness you're open!"

He moved aside and allowed her to step inside, out of the rain. Wearily setting down her bag, Morgan eased herself onto an old wooden kitchen chair set against the wall.

"My car broke down back there on the highway. About two miles from here. The battery is dead, I think. Can you fix it?" she asked.

"I can try. I have the only gas station in town," he said cheerfully. "There's a young fellow in town who gives me a hand. He's a pretty good mechanic. We'll go take a look at it in the morning. Where are you headed?" He was studying her while he spoke. This slim, bedraggled figure was not someone he had seen in town before. Her accent assured him she was an American.

"Hidden Island," she said. "Do you know it?"

"Yes. About a mile off the coast," he said. "You missed the last ferry. It left an hour ago."

"Oh no!" she moaned.

Her letter of acceptance had listed the summer schedule of the ferry. Morgan realized with a sinking heart that she had barely skimmed over that information in her excitement at being hired. Her disappointment was written on her face.

"Is there some place in this town I could spend the night?" she asked.

The old man scratched his head. "Well, there is a small inn. We don't get many tourists in Port Elgin. Most of them prefer to take the ferry to Prince Edward Island," he said. Then, seeing her forlorn expression, he added hastily, "Don't worry, miss. Old Joe will run you over to the island in the launch. I'll ring him up."

Morgan clenched her hands in her lap while the old man made the phone call from a back room. Whoever Old Joe was, she hoped he would be available to take her to her final destination. She was mentally counting how much money was left in her account. With the car in need of repair, she didn't want to pay for a room at an inn if she didn't have to, especially with the end of her journey so near.

A few minutes later the man returned, smiling. "Just follow this street to the end. Turn left and go all the way down to the wharf. You'll see a big motor launch. Joe will have the running lights on. You can't miss it." He looked apologetic. "Sorry I can't drive you in this rain, but I can't leave the station alone."

"I understand," she said. "It's all right. My clothes are already soaked. Another walk in the rain won't matter."

"If you'll leave the key to your car, miss, we'll get it tomorrow," he offered.

"That's great." Morgan twisted the key from her ring and handed it to the old man. "Thank you. I don't know when I'll be able to get back here, though." She thought for a moment, undecided. "I guess, if the battery can be recharged, do it. If you have to replace it, well—" she shrugged, "I'll need my car to get back home when my job is finished. If you have to put in a new battery, do it. I'll pay you whenever I get back to town. But if there's something more that has to be repaired, you'd better wait until you check with me first." She smiled wryly. "I can't afford anything more just yet." She lowered her eyes in embarrassment.

The old man patted her arm reassuringly. "All right, miss. That's fine. Now, write down your name and home address for me. There's no phone on Hidden Island, so I'll just have to wait until I hear from you if there's any decision to be made about your car."

Morgan wrote on a slip of paper, then turned and extended her hand. "Thank you, Mr. . . ."

"Gagnon. Alphonse Gagnon," he said.

"Thank you, Mr. Gagnon. I'm Morgan Anders."

"It's nice to meet you, Miss Anders," he said. "You're an American, eh? Where's your home?"

"New York," she replied. "I've come here for the summer to work on Hidden Island."

"Well, good night, Miss Anders," he said. "And good luck."

She stepped once more into the pouring rain and followed his directions.

Nearing the wharf, Morgan wrinkled her nose at the strong odor of fish and the damp, musky smell of the lake. As she drew nearer, the overpowering smell of diesel fuel blotted out all others. Before she saw the lights of the launch, Morgan could hear the powerful engines throbbing in the darkness. As she drew closer, she could make out the figure of a man standing at the wheel.

He walked to the side of the boat and reached out his hand for her overnight bag. Setting it down on board, he again stretched out his hand and helped her aboard. Up close, Morgan observed a thatch of white hair and wrinkled, parchment skin.

"Evening, miss. Hidden Island, is it?" he greeted her.

Again she noticed the lyrical French accent. "Yes. And I'm grateful that you're willing to take me over so late," she said, smiling and glancing around the launch.

The storm had blown over, leaving a steady, driving rain. The old man's eyes narrowed as Morgan shivered. From under a seat, he produced a drab blanket.

"Here, miss, wrap yourself in this. It'll be a cold ride in this weather."

Morgan gratefully accepted the blanket and huddled on the seat, exposed to the wind and rain. There was no cabin and no way to get comfortable. She would have to make the best of it and hope the ride was over quickly. The thought of hot food and a dry bed at the end of her journey lifted her spirits.

The boat eased from the dock and moved slowly into open water. Then, with a deafening roar, it picked up speed and skittered across the waves. Morgan bowed her head and wrapped the blanket tighter about her. Each time the boat danced off a wave, her stomach seemed to meet her chest with bone-crushing force. Numbly, she gripped the chipped, wooden seat and held on tightly. She was glad the engines were too loud to allow conversation. All she wanted now was to feel land beneath her feet once more.

Morgan couldn't imagine how the old man knew where he was headed. Even when the motor launch pulled up to a tiny strip of land, Morgan could barely make out a pinpoint of light in the distance. When the engines were switched off, it took her a moment to adjust to the silence.

"Are there many houses on Hidden Island?" she asked.

"None. Just the Taylor lodge," he said.

"Is that the light I see?" Morgan pointed in the direction of the light.

"Yes. You're expected, are you, miss?"

"Well, I'm not sure they expect me tonight. But they do expect me sometime soon," she said doubtfully.

The old man stooped and picked up her overnight case. Leaping with ease onto the long, wooden dock, he set down the case and reached out for Morgan's hand.

She smiled up through the rain at the old man. "Are you coming with me?" she asked hopefully.

"No, miss. I'll leave you here," he said, turning toward his boat. "Just keep walking straight toward that light. And watch your step in the dark," he cautioned.

"Don't I owe you anything for this trip?" she called to his retreating back.

"Not a thing. Good night, miss."

"Thank you. Good night."

Morgan picked up the bag and trudged through tall, dripping weeds and dark clusters of trees toward the light. Without warning, she lost her footing and sank in mud to her knees. Off-balance, the overnight bag dropped from her hands, sinking up to its handles in thick ooze. As she began to fall forward, her arms flailed about wildly. Her fingers brushed the low-hanging branch of a tree, and the weight of the branch saved her from falling on her face.

With her breath coming in short gasps of panic, Morgan suddenly recalled all the frightening childhood stories she had heard about quicksand. Forcing herself to stand perfectly still, she realized in a few moments that she was definitely not sinking. Gripping the muddy handle of her overnight bag, she pulled her weight against the tree limb and climbed slowly out of the muddy ditch. As she continued walking, every blackened silhouette of a tree looked like some grotesque creature looming up to threaten her. The wind sighed in the trees, causing the hair on the back of her neck to prickle in fear.

After another hundred yards or so, the light seemed much nearer. Thank goodness she had made it, she thought. Drawing near the lodge, she could smell smoke. A fireplace. How lovely. Warmth. Dry clothes. A soft bed. Safety.

She climbed wide, wooden stairs and knocked on a rough-hewn wood door. After a long wait, the door was thrown open and a tall figure stood bathed in the light from within.

He surveyed her silently, taking in the long strings of hair plastered to her cheeks, the soaked jacket and jeans and the rivers of mud trickling down from her knees to her feet.

"Yes?" The deep masculine voice had the definite ring of anger.

"I'm here for the job," Morgan said uneasily, secretly cursing herself for choking on her voice.

"Sorry. I'm not in the market for budding starlets. How did you get here? Swim?" His eyes skimmed over her mud-soaked figure. "Or crawl?" he added contemptuously.

Morgan's mouth dropped open, and she stared, speechless, at the imposing figure. He was closing the door on her. Her hand shot out, pushing against the rough wood.

"Now wait a minute!" she shouted above the wind. "I came here for a job. If you'll give me a moment, I'll show you the letter."

As he paused, Morgan dropped the overnight bag and unzipped it, fishing through her purse for the letter and map. Triumphantly, she held it up for his inspection.

"Here it is. See!"

The paper was snatched from her hands, and as the man half-turned to read the letter, Morgan studied his craggy profile in the path of light. At five and a half feet, Morgan thought of herself as average in height, but this man towered above her. He was well over six feet tall. Tousled, blond hair spilled across a wide forehead. Dressed in a rumpled shirt and faded jeans, his feet bare, he appeared to be furious at this late-hour interruption. His chin and neck were shadowed with a growth of scraggly red-gold hair.

The man shot her an incredulous look. "You are Morgan Anders?"

"Yes," she said, lifting her chin defiantly. Now maybe he would let her in out of the rain.

Instead, he returned the letter to her and said coldly, "How did you get here?"

"A man brought me in a launch. Old Joe, I believe he's called."

"Has the launch left the island?"

"Yes. He pointed out the direction I should take and left. Why?"

He moved stiffly aside and said grimly, "I suppose you'll have to spend the night. There's no way back now. I'll signal for the ferry to stop for you in the morning."

"Go back?" Morgan stepped hesitantly inside and dropped the overnight bag in the foyer. She was shivering violently, and she could hear the crackle of a fire nearby. The man followed her glance, then stared down at her shoes, which were dripping muddy water on the wooden floor.

"You'll have to get out of those wet things. Is this all you brought with you?" he asked, indicating the small bag.

"Yes. My car broke down on the highway outside of Port Elgin. I had to leave my luggage behind."

He turned his back on her and said over his shoulder, "Follow me through here."

He led her to a bedroom and indicated a bathroom beyond. "You can shower in there. I'll look around for something for you to wear." He turned toward the door, then stopped as if just remembering something else. "When did you eat?"

"Hours ago. Lunch, I guess." She stood in the same spot, crushed by the coldness of his tone.

"I'll find something," he said brusquely. He walked away, closing the door firmly behind him.

Morgan stared at the closed door, puzzled by the man's obvious anger. What had she interrupted? He seemed to be alone here. Maybe he had been asleep and always awoke like a bear. Judging by his rumpled appearance, he wasn't expecting anyone to disturb his solitude tonight. Maybe he was a caretaker here and didn't want to have to entertain her until the owners returned. She shrugged off her questions and walked to the bathroom. Stripping off her soaked clothing, Morgan climbed gratefully beneath the hot shower. When she emerged from the steaming bathroom, an oversized robe was draped across the foot of the bed. She toweled her hair dry and shrugged into the robe, cinching the waist and staring resignedly at the excess material ballooning about her wrists and ankles.

The strong odor of coffee led her to the kitchen. She wrinkled her nose at the smell of something burning as she pushed open the door. The man turned and regarded her silently, taking in her waves of dark hair and the slim figure engulfed in the robe. Then he popped up two pieces of burned toast from a toaster, sending a trail of black smoke curling toward the ceiling.

"This will have to do," he said curtly, dumping a mass of overdone scrambled eggs on her plate.

Morgan began to eat mechanically. It wouldn't have mattered if he had given her cardboard. She was so hungry, she would have eaten anything. With her knife, she scraped the toast until it was edible. Wrapping her hands around the coffee cup, she sipped gratefully at the strong, black brew. When she cleaned her plate, Morgan sat back, feeling her strength slowly return.

The man had stayed at the sink during the entire time, taking out his fury on the pots and pans. Morgan moved up beside him to rinse her dishes in the sink.

"Thank you," she said quietly.

Ignoring her, the man dried his hands on a kitchen towel, then turned and stalked from the room.

Morgan left her dishes in the sink and followed him.

In the living room she found him standing by the huge stone fireplace, his arm resting on the mantel, staring moodily into the flames.

"I realize my arrival tonight has inconvenienced you," she said, vainly fighting to control the anger she felt at this man's arrogant attitude. "But I'm sure that when Mr. Taylor returns he'll confirm my letter of employment."

The man turned and regarded her. Strange, tawny eyes reflecting the glow of the fire caught and held her gaze.

In a barely concealed rage, he said, "I am Kent Taylor. And you, miss, are a cheat and a fraud and a liar!"

"What!" Morgan's mouth dropped open. She was

too stunned to say more. This horrible man was her employer.

"I checked your references thoroughly," he said in an icy tone. "Nowhere did anyone bother to mention that you were female."

Morgan drew herself up to her full height, looking slightly ridiculous in the oversized robe, and said haughtily, "I don't see that my sex has any bearing on this at all."

"Really!" His eyes blazed. "Then I suppose you can explain why you never bothered to mention in your letter of application that you were a woman. I had specifically instructed my secretary to screen all the applications for a man who could endure the rigors of a summer on this deserted island. In no way did you give any indication that you were female."

Morgan stared at him without speaking for what seemed to be a full minute. Then, tearing her gaze from his, she walked to the window and stared out at the blackness. She had never considered the possibility that he had expected her to be a man. She had just been so delighted to find something that sounded interesting and challenging. But, she reminded herself sadly, her first name often confused people. She dropped her head and stood with her hands clenched nervously at her sides.

In a barely audible tone she said, "I see. You wanted a man." Turning, she lifted her chin defiantly and added, "I'm sorry. I really didn't mean to deceive you. It never occurred to me that you were looking for a man. I just saw your ad and impulsively wrote for the job."

His eyes narrowed angrily. "How convenient! And when I checked your references, Fairfield Academy just happened to be a boys' school. And the Wanaway Camp just happened to be a boys' summer camp." He glowered at her. "Sorry. I can't buy your story."

Morgan clamped her hands on her hips and returned his glare. "Well, it's the truth. I didn't mean to deceive you. I do work for a boys' school. And for the past three summers I worked at Wanaway. And if you got the wrong impression, I can't help it. Right now I'm too tired to care what you think."

He shot her a murderous look and then said quietly, "I'm sure you can find your way to your room, Miss Anders. I'll signal for the ferry to pick you up in the morning."

Morgan spit the words boldly with more bravado than she really felt. "By all means! I'll leave in the morning. But you'll have to cover my travel expenses. My car needs repair, and I have no money left. It took all I had to get here." Morgan fought to hold back the tears of frustration that were threatening to erupt.

Kent Taylor watched her outburst in stony silence.

She turned on her heel and strode angrily from the room. In the bedroom she stripped off the clumsy robe and climbed beneath the soft blankets.

What a mess! What a terrible mess! She already had passed up the job at Wanaway Camp for this. Now she would have no income at all for the summer. Without this job, she couldn't make it. She couldn't even go back to her apartment in the city. When she had received notification of this job for the summer, she had sublet her apartment to one of the teachers from Fairfield who had accepted an offer to teach summer classes at a nearby public school. She had thought herself so lucky. A high-salaried position for the summer. Someone paying her rent. By fall she would have saved enough for a new compact car. What in the world would she do now?

Before Morgan fell into an exhausted sleep, she noticed that the light still burned in the other room, and she could hear the man pacing back and forth like a caged lion.

Chapter Two

Sunlight streamed through the cracks of the wooden blinds, spilling across the slim form of the girl in the narrow bed. Morgan turned and gravitated toward the spot of warmth. Abruptly, her eyes fluttered open, and she sat bolt upright in the bed as she recalled the ugly scene of the night before.

She had wrestled with her dilemma before sleep overtook her, but she had come up with no solution. She would just have to return to New York and hope to find some job to tide her over until the start of school and her return to the Fairfield Academy office. She had no idea where she would stay. There were several friends she could call on. Hopefully, one of them would be willing to put her up until her apartment was vacated in August.

In the bathroom Morgan stepped over the pile of

sodden clothes she had dropped the previous night. After a quick shower, she dressed in the shorts and cotton shirt she had stuffed into the overnight bag. Her thick, dark hair had dried overnight, falling into soft natural waves that bounced about her shoulders. She ran a brush through the tangles and picked up the pile of clothes. A quick search in the back of the lodge led her to a small laundry room. She piled the clothes in the washer. While the machine whirred, she looked around for a dryer. Apparently the room was only large enough to accommodate the small washer. Morgan shrugged. The clothes would dry just as well in the fresh air. When the cycle ended, she carried her clothes out the back door. Within a few minutes the porch railing and tree branches nearby were gaily decorated with flapping jeans and a flannel shirt and jacket as well as several filmy underthings. Morgan set her damp sneakers on the steps of the back porch to dry in the sun.

Padding through the kitchen in bare feet, Morgan opened the refrigerator. She had decided, while hanging her clothes, that if that monster in the other room was going to send her back empty-handed, the least he could do was provide her with a decent meal. The condemned man ate a hearty meal. She frowned at the thought and carried eggs, milk, cheese, ham and an onion to the counter. She searched around the sunny kitchen. In a drawer under the stove she found some pots and pans. Selecting a skillet, she set to work. After that awful meal last night, this omelet was going to be perfect. She carefully watched the toast, taking it from the toaster at just the right moment. As she skillfully turned the eggs and watched the cheese melt, she began to hum to herself.

Despite all the things that had gone wrong on this trip, she was determined to find something optimistic to cling to. There had been real disasters in her life, and she had managed to survive them. She paused in her movement and grimaced. Well, she had survived them, more or less. The truth was, she really needed this summer job to survive. She had considered herself so lucky when the letter confirming her employment had arrived. This was the light at the end of that long tunnel of scrimping and saving. And now, the light had been extinguished.

Buttering the toast, Morgan groped for a hopeful thought to brighten her morning. A glance out the window assured her that the sun was shining. A good day for a long drive. That thought should cheer her, but instead, Morgan groaned. She hated thinking about the weary drive back to New York, with no place to stay at the end of the journey. There must be something pleasant to think about. Why spoil a perfectly good breakfast with gloomy thoughts? A grin curled her lips. She had suddenly thought of something that made her smile. She would love to tell Mr. Kent Taylor just what she thought of him. How dare he permit her to drive six hundred miles for nothing! How dare he suggest that only a man could do an adequate job for him! Morgan smiled. Just thinking about what she would like to say to him made her feel better. She would enjoy this breakfast after all.

When everything was ready, she carried her plate to the other room. She had noticed an oak table set in a bay window with a beautiful view of the Northumberland Strait, which separated this island from the mainland. She intended to enjoy this meal in a pleasant setting.

Just as she arranged her plate on a bright yellow placemat and picked up her fork, she heard the kettle whistling in the kitchen. She scurried away to make herself a cup of instant coffee.

A thorough search of the cupboards revealed no coffee. She wasted several minutes rummaging through every cupboard and drawer. Finally she settled for a cup of tea. Carrying the steaming cup to the table, she stopped in her tracks. Kent Taylor was sitting at her place at the table, calmly eating her omelet.

"That's my breakfast!" she hissed.

He looked up, fork in midair, then took another bite of the omelet. "It's not bad," he remarked, and bit into a piece of toast spread with jam.

"Not bad? It's perfect! And I made it for myself," she said, setting down the cup of tea and reaching over for her plate.

"You can't blame me for eating it," he growled. "It was set at my place at the table."

"Your place or not, I don't make it a habit of getting up early to prepare breakfast for strangers," she said angrily, grabbing the plate just as he speared another forkful.

"Listen," he said, savoring the taste, "I'll make you a deal. Since I've already started eating this, I'll finish and then make you some scrambled eggs. Deal?"

Morgan's eyes grew round. She couldn't believe what she was hearing. "Not a chance! If last night was a fair sample, I'd say your cooking leaves much to be desired. In fact, Mr. Taylor," and she glowered at him across the table as she said the words deliberately, "to be as blunt as you seem to enjoy being, I'd say that your cooking stinks!"

She bent her head and took a bite of the omelet, feeling his eyes boring into her as she did. Calmly, she broke off a piece of toast and nibbled it. She glanced in his direction. He was still staring at her.

Darn it! she thought. Taking another bite, she cast a furtive glance in his direction. His eyes were fastened on her. She felt too self-conscious even to enjoy this beautiful meal. Finally, to ease the situation, she surrendered. With a sigh of defeat, she reached for her saucer and divided the omelet in half.

With a smile of triumph, Kent Taylor accepted it and rushed to the kitchen for a fork and a glass of milk. For the next few minutes, they both silently enjoyed their food, making no attempt at conversation.

When at last Morgan leaned back and sipped her tea, she allowed her gaze to roam across the vast stretches of water outside the window. Golden sunlight danced across the waves. Foam spread along a white, sandy shore.

"This is such a beautiful place," she sighed contentedly. "Do you come here every summer?"

"No. And I don't come here for the beauty," he snapped. "I come here for the solitude."

"Oh." She understood his message. He wasn't interested in being pleasant or in making any attempt at casual conversation. He wanted to be rid of her.

Picking up her dishes, she walked quickly to the kitchen. Kent Taylor followed her, carrying the saucer and yellow placemat.

In a quieter tone, he said, "Look, Miss Anders. I thought about what you said last night. About not realizing that I had thought I hired a male secretary. I believe you."

She turned and stared at him.

With a wicked grin, he added, "The whole thing—the boys' academy, the boys' summer camp, the unusual name—has the ring of truth to it. It's too dumb to be something you just made up."

"Well, thank you for accepting my dumb excuse!" she retorted sarcastically. "As a matter of fact, I should have been suspicious when I saw the salary you were offering. Obviously, you believe a man should be paid much more than a woman. That's higher than anything I've ever been offered. I knew it was too good to be true!"

Angrily, she turned her back on him and began to wash her dishes, clattering them noisily to release her tension.

Kent Taylor muttered an oath and began to leave the room, then paused and returned to tower above her. "For your information, Miss Anders, that is exactly the salary I pay my regular secretary. I'm a very demanding boss, and I expect a great deal of work from my secretary. So I have to pay accordingly."

She glanced at him sideways and asked, "And what happened to your regular secretary?"

"Helen's daughter is having her first baby, and she wanted to be with her. She's gone to Seattle for the summer. Rather than lose her completely, I agreed to the leave of absence."

"Helen," Morgan said with emphasis. "What a funny name for a man."

"Stop being nasty, Miss Anders," he snapped.

"I'll be anything I want to be, Mr. Taylor. Since you are not paying my salary, you can't tell me what to do."

He strode across the room, then stopped abruptly at the window. Morgan followed his gaze and realized in humiliation just what had caught his eye. A lacey bra had blown off its perch on the branch of the tree and had snagged on a latch outside the window. It bobbed up and down on a current of wind. Kent turned and raised an eyebrow in question.

Feeling the heat rise to her cheeks, Morgan said quickly, "I used your washer this morning. I couldn't find a dryer, so I hung my things outside. My—it must have blown off the tree branch."

"How inventive, Miss Anders," he said dryly. He turned and studied the filmy bra, then added, "Well, are you going out to catch it or watch while it blows across the Northumberland Strait all the way to Port Elgin? That would give the tourists something to talk about."

Without another word, he scowled and left, slamming the door behind him.

Morgan hurried outside to retrieve her things before they all blew away. A short time later, as she walked down the hall to pack her overnight case, she stopped in surprise outside the open door of Kent's room. It looked as though a hurricane had struck. There were papers everywhere. Some were wadded up and tossed under the bed. Some were crumpled, some torn. Morgan stared in astonishment.

Kent Taylor picked up a pile of papers from his table and began to carry them to a desk. As he slipped on a sheet of paper on the floor beneath his feet, the pile of pages dropped from his hands, scattering everywhere.

Suppressing a laugh, Morgan walked in and began to help him straighten up the mass of papers. "What in the world is all this?" she asked.

"This is my work—or what's left of it," he muttered angrily.

Morgan picked up a sheet of paper and studied it. Words were crossed out. Others were circled with red ink. On another page she noticed huge sections marked off in squares and boxes. Much of the writing was barely legible.

"If this is a sample of what you do, Mr. Taylor," she said earnestly, "I'm afraid you're not going to be very successful."

Despite his obvious agitation, Kent's lips curled in a half-smile. "It is a mess, isn't it?" he remarked. Then, setting down the papers he had collected, he turned to her. "This is why I have to pay such an outrageous salary to keep a secretary. My writing is scribble. My typing isn't much better. And when I'm working, I just keep on going, no matter how many pages I cross out or throw away."

"Just what is it you do, Mr. Taylor?" Morgan asked.

He studied her for a moment as though weighing her question. Then, with a shrug, he said, "Right now, I'm writing a screenplay for a film that Reynolds Standish will direct. And it has to be ready by the end of August."

Morgan caught her breath. Reynolds Standish was probably the most acclaimed director in Hollywood. And this man was writing a screenplay for his direction. At least now Morgan understood Kent's need for a competent secretary. Lost in her own thoughts, Morgan neatly dropped the papers on his desk and quietly left the room.

An hour later she carried the overnight bag out to the front porch. Then she circled the lodge and picked up her sneakers from the back steps, where they had thoroughly dried in the sun.

After putting on her shoes, she straightened and saw Kent running a yellow flag up the flagpole atop the lodge.

Shielding her eyes from the sun, she shouted, "What's that for?"

He stared down at her from the balcony and replied, "That's the signal I send up when I want the ferry to stop here."

Clever, she thought. This island really was isolated. She had seen no telephone. There were no other residents. Just a series of signals to the mainland.

What would Kent Taylor do if he were injured? How would he get help? She shrugged. It was none of her business. In a little while she would leave here and head back to the dirt and grime and humidity of the city. She frowned, lost in thought. Other summers she had escaped to Wanaway Camp. The pay was very little, compared with this. But there were clean lakes and shaded bridle paths for the horses stabled nearby and fresh air and sunshine. Now she would return to New York. Her frown deepened. That is, if her car made it.

Morgan walked some distance from the lodge through waist-high growth and stooped to pick a wild rose. Pale pink in color, with a deep rose center, it gave off a delicate fragrance. She absently tucked it behind her ear and walked on toward the shore. The clusters of trees, which last night had seemed so dark and threatening, were viewed now as they really were. Soft cottonwoods, with their delicate silvery leaves, grew in clumps on the eastern edge of the island. Further inland, there were lovely red maple and towering pine and blue spruce. Along the shore, several odd-shaped stones, worn smooth as glass and bleached by the sun, caught her eye, and she bent and picked them up. A little further on she noticed a pretty shell and scooped it up. As she walked slowly back toward the lodge, she put all her treasures in her pocket.

The peace of the island was soothing. She sighed. It would have been a fine place to spend the summer. As she climbed the broad, wooden steps to the porch, Kent hurried out the door.

"The ferry is coming," he said curtly.

Morgan turned and watched as the huge boat came into view. Kent lifted her overnight bag and walked in the direction from which she had come the night before. Morgan followed along the long, wooden dock that had been built in the shallow water. In a short time the ferry stopped, and a wooden ramp dropped down. Morgan turned to Kent Taylor and extended her hand. Instead of handing her the bag, he took her by the elbow and helped her aboard.

"I didn't realize you were coming with me," she said.

"I have some supplies to pick up in town," he said briskly. Without another word, he walked to the far railing of the huge ferry.

Morgan stood at the railing and tried to relax, determined to enjoy the view. The breeze ruffled her hair, blowing the forgotten rose away. As she looked up, Kent Taylor reached out and caught it as it blew past him. He inhaled the fragrance, then absently dropped it into the churning water below. Morgan shrugged and turned away.

Overhead, gulls soared on the breezes, then dipped and snatched their breakfast of unsuspecting fish from the waters of the Northumberland Strait. Morgan moved to the far railing to watch the lobster boats in the distance with flocks of gulls hovering about their decks. Across the strait, at the shore of Prince Edward Island, there towered incredible red cliffs. Even the water took on the red hue from the cliffs and sand and soil along the shore.

As the ferry neared Port Elgin, in New Brunswick, it passed quiet coves and inlets dotted with deserted, unspoiled beaches. Morgan thought what an adventure it would be to explore the coves and tunnels of rock they were passing. Then, sadly, she lowered her head and pondered what lay ahead of her. It would be at least a twelve- or fourteen-hour drive back to New York. And at the end of the journey there would be no place to stay. She frowned as she thought of the steamy, impatient city in the summer: air conditioners that quit during a heat wave; hot, irritable crowds surging along teeming sidewalks; jobs by the thousands being snatched up by the college students home for summer holiday. She would be lucky to get waitress work in a diner. Or maybe a job as a clerk in one of the big department stores. She would have to find a place to stay right away. If she had to pay for a room for very long, she would deplete her meager savings.

As all these troubling thoughts tormented her, Morgan stared down at the swirling waters below and gripped the rail tightly. That beautiful promise of hope that she had savored on the exhausting drive here was gone, dashed like the waves against the savage cliffs. Still frowning, she turned away suddenly without seeing Kent Taylor, who was leaning against the railing, watching her intently.

With a deafening blast on the horn, the ferry docked at Port Elgin. Dozens of vehicles, picked up at Prince Edward Island and neighboring islands, drove down the broad ramp. Then the passengers walked down the ramp. All about her the crowds of tourists and summer residents had a festive air. Morgan snatched up her overnight bag and followed the crowd. She could make out Kent's tall figure far ahead. When he reached the street, he turned and waited for her.

"Where did you leave your car?" he asked.

"I left it back on the highway, but I gave my key to Mr. Gagnon at the gas station. He promised to bring it in for repair."

Kent looked at her with new interest. "You think of everything, don't you, Miss Anders?"

"I have to, Mr. Taylor," she said dryly. "If I don't, who will?"

"Oh, I'm sure you have scores of men at your beck and call, just waiting to hear your pleasure," he said with mock sarcasm.

"Well, you're wrong," she snapped. "I can take care of myself."

He turned and regarded her for a moment, seeing the defiant jut of her chin, the tightly clenched jaw. Then he said, "Sorry. I didn't realize it was a sore spot."

They walked along the street in silence until they came to the gas station. Alphonse Gagnon was pumping gas, and he looked up smiling as he saw Morgan.

"Well, Miss Anders. It didn't take you long to get back to town," he called.

"Not as long as I expected it would," she said with meaning.

Kent watched this exchange silently.

"Would you like to give me the news, Mr. Gagnon?" she asked hopefully.

"Well," he said, grinning, "like they say, I've got some good news and some bad news, Miss Anders. Which would you like first?"

Morgan sighed. "I gather it wasn't my battery?"

"Oh, yes, it was the battery, among other things," he said.

"What other things?" she asked, feeling her spirits sinking.

"We have to replace the battery. Yours was just too old to recharge. But that isn't the bad news. There seems to be a short in the starter. That's why the car wouldn't start. And it was a drain on the battery, making it wear out even sooner."

"Can you fix the starter?" Morgan asked.

"Yes, but I'll have to send to the States for the parts."

"How long will it take?" Morgan asked.

"Can't say. Maybe a week. Maybe longer," the old man said.

"A week," Morgan muttered.

"Or longer," Kent cut in. "Is that your car over there?" he asked, pointing to her car parked alongside the service garage.

"Yes," she said without enthusiasm.

"I don't think it's worth repairing," he said coldly. "Why not just invest in a new one?"

Morgan turned and fixed him with a look of cold fury. "That's what I intend to do when I earn enough money. In the meantime, Mr. Taylor, not all of us can just run out and replace all the things that wear out."

"Sorry. I didn't mean to sound so . . . arrogant," he said. "But I do feel you'll be wasting your money on that old car."

"How much will it cost me, Mr. Gagnon?" Morgan asked, deliberately ignoring Kent.

"Come on in the station and I'll figure it out," he offered.

Morgan followed him inside the station, with Kent trailing behind them. When the old man handed her the written estimate, she gritted her teeth.

"All right, Mr. Gagnon. I don't have any choice. Go ahead and replace the battery, but I'll have to take my chances on the starter. If it gets me back to New York, I'll have it taken care of there whenever I can. How long will it take to replace the battery?"

"I should have that ready in an hour or two," he told her. "But you really shouldn't take a chance driving all that way with a faulty starter. You could end up stranded on some deserted highway like you did last night," he warned.

"Thank you, Mr. Gagnon," she said. "But I really have no choice." Morgan walked dejectedly from the station and set her overnight bag in the back seat of her car.

A few minutes later Kent walked outside and joined her. "Miss Anders," he said, "there's a diner down the street. Let's grab a cup of coffee."

Distracted by thoughts of her car and the long drive ahead of her, Morgan allowed herself to be led away. As they entered the small diner, an old woman standing behind the counter smiled a greeting. In the kitchen an old man wearing a chef's hat was busy at the grill. Morgan and Kent took a seat at a booth, and a young girl of about fourteen or fifteen, dressed in shorts and a T-shirt, approached with a menu.

"Just coffee for both of us, please," Kent Taylor said.

"Two coffees, Gramps," the girl called.

At that, Morgan's face fell as though she were about to cry. She bit her lower lip painfully to keep it from quivering. As she regained her composure, Kent studied her.

"What's wrong, Miss Anders?" He was genuinely concerned.

"Nothing," she said, trying to shrug off her feelings. "It just startled me to hear that young girl call him Gramps," she said. "I used to call my grandfather that."

"Used to," he repeated.

"Gramps died last year." She stared down at the tabletop. "He was all the family I ever knew. He raised me."

"I see." Kent stared at her bowed head. "Is that why you're so annoyingly independent?"

"What!" she said, so startled and angry at his words that she suddenly forgot her sorrow.

"Morgan Anders, you're not like any other woman. The women I've known wouldn't have the slightest idea of how to deal with a car that quit on a lonely road or what to do if the promise of a job at the end of hundreds of miles turned out all wrong."

She stared at the tabletop, tracing the grain of wood with her finger, saying nothing. She suddenly felt too drained to even argue with him.

As the young waitress set down two mugs of coffee, Kent cleared his throat. "Miss Anders, I'd like to make you a proposition," he said quietly.

Morgan looked up sharply, suspicious of his tone.

"I need a secretary right away. I really think it's too late to start looking for someone else now. By

43

the time I place another ad and check out references, the summer will be half over. And I'm
working on a tight deadline. Also, you need time to
get your car in proper working order."

Morgan studied his face. He seemed earnest, but
she smarted when she recalled the frigid reception
upon her arrival.

"I thought you wanted a male secretary," she
said, bristling.

"I did, blast it!" he said. "But time is flying. I have
to get this screenplay ready now. I don't have time to
fool around checking out references at this late date.
Besides, I only specified a male secretary because I
didn't want to be bothered by some helpless female
trying to adjust to life on a secluded island. You
don't strike me as being at all helpless. I expect you
can take care of yourself," he added dryly.

"And the salary?" she demanded. She had decided she didn't really like Kent Taylor, and she was
unwilling to back down now.

In an even tone he said, "The salary will be what
was listed in the ad."

Their eyes met across the table, and Kent added,
"Before you make any decisions, Miss Anders, I had
better point out a few facts. First of all, my work
doesn't follow any particular schedule. In fact, I
keep crazy hours. When everything is going right, I
might work right through the night and on into the
next day. I always work late at night and sleep during
the mornings. But I've been known to work for two
or three days without stopping, then drop wherever I
am and sleep around the clock. I can't stand any
interruptions, which is why I'm at Hidden Island. I

can't stand a telephone, television, radio or visitors when I'm feeling like working. I'm moody, cranky, demanding, and an absolute bear when things are going wrong. I'll expect you to decipher my scribbled pages and follow my orders, even retyping everything if I change my mind. And I'll want it all done as quickly as possible so I can read what I wrote and edit it before going on to the next scene."

Morgan stared into his amber eyes, seeing the anger and frustration and impatience gleaming there. She had no doubt that he meant every word. As he turned to look out the window, Morgan studied his stern profile. His nostrils flared in anger. His eyes narrowed as they searched, not the people passing by, nor the few cars driving slowly along the main street, but beyond the town, toward the wide expanse of water. Morgan knew that even while he sat here in the diner with her, his thoughts were of the island and the work waiting to be done.

He returned his gaze to her and caught her studying him openly. Boldly, he returned the stare, peering into her dark brown eyes, seeing the thick, dark lashes suddenly lower in defense.

Morgan felt a flush of heat rush to her face. This man was too arrogant even to have the decency to look away. He continued to stare at her, seeming to enjoy her confusion. She turned to stare out the window, searching for something on which to concentrate for a moment until her embarrassment passed. When she looked back at him, he was still watching her.

"I don't have time for the social graces, Miss Anders. I don't shave for days at a time. I don't care what clothes I wear. Sometimes I forget to eat. And if you make a mistake, I'll take your head off. If I need to, I'll make you work around the clock, too. By the time this job is finished, you'll hate me, Miss Anders. And I won't care. All I care about is getting this screenplay finished on time." His eyes held hers. "Think you can handle it?"

Morgan heard the challenge in his tone and knew she wanted to prove to him that she could meet it.

With mock sarcasm, she said, "You make it sound so attractive; how can I resist?" Then she added, with an edge to her voice, "But I really have no choice."

"Neither do I," he retorted.

Morgan had come too far to back away from his offer now. She ran her hand distractedly through her thick mane of hair. She didn't like this man, and she couldn't imagine being forced to spend an entire summer with him on a lonely island. But the alternative was much worse. If she refused his offer, she had to face the long drive back to New York. And at the end of the journey, she faced no job and no place to stay.

With narrowed eyes, Kent Taylor watched her closely as she agonized over her decision.

Solemnly, she extended her hand across the table. He stared at it for a moment, then crushed her small hand in his large one in a formal handshake.

Without a pause, he stood abruptly and said, "Well, then, with that out of the way, we have work to do. We'll pick up some groceries at the store, then stop by the garage for your luggage."

Morgan followed his impatient gait from the diner

46

and down the street to the store. He was in such a hurry that he was nearly half a block ahead of her.

Later, at the gas station, she said, "I'll tell Mr. Gagnon to go ahead and order the parts for my starter."

"There's no need to," Kent said smugly. "I already told him to earlier."

"You what!" Morgan asked indignantly. She couldn't believe he would actually have taken matters into his own hands without even the courtesy of consulting her first.

"Mr. Taylor, how could you be so sure I would accept your offer?" she asked through gritted teeth.

"I figured you would," he said. "There's no way that car of yours could make it to New York in the shape it's in. This was the only sensible thing to do," he said calmly. "Now, get your luggage out of the trunk and let's get moving. We can still make the early ferry."

Morgan's eyes narrowed in anger. "Don't you ever presume to make my decisions for me again, Mr. Taylor. I told you before, I can take care of myself!" she hissed as she strode toward her car.

A hint of a smile played on his lips as he watched her.

A few minutes later, Morgan and Kent struggled under the weight of her luggage and his grocery bags. Safely settled on the ferry, Morgan sat down gratefully at the railing and watched as the tiny outline of Hidden Island came into view on the horizon. The waters of the Northumberland Strait were a deep blue, then further out, a brilliant turquoise. In the distance, the water became an incredible red, reflecting the magnificent cliffs and sand along the shore of Prince Edward Island. Morgan shivered in anticipation. She didn't have to leave this fabulous Canadian paradise after all. She would be free to roam the tiny, green island and maybe even explore the coastal towns of New Brunswick and the quiet coves of Prince Edward Island before she left.

She stole a quick glance at the imposing figure of the man at the railing waiting impatiently to get back to his lodge and his work. The stern set of his shoulders reminded her yet again that she had struck a bargain with a very demanding man. A bargain she may yet live to regret.

Chapter Three

Upon their return to the island, Kent explained Morgan's duties to her, quickly but carefully going over the system he had worked out. Warily, Morgan leaned over his shoulder as he spoke, listening attentively to his explanations and wondering if she would ever be able to make any sense of it all. It seemed a maze of paperwork.

He turned and studied her face for a moment. "You do understand what I want, don't you?" he asked.

Instinctively, Morgan backed away from him. She could tell by his tone that he was impatient with all these explanations. Like a racehorse straining at the starting gate, Kent Taylor struggled to get through the tedious instructions in order to return to the work he really cared about—the actual writing of his screenplay.

She noted the tiny furrows lining his forehead. Absently he passed his hand across his brow as though to wipe away the visible trace of frustration.

"I guess I understand most of what you've told me. I'm sure I'll have a lot of questions as I work my way through this mountain of typing," she said gravely. "But I'm beginning to see a pattern in all of this."

"Good. By the way, Morgan," he said, "we'll be working and living so closely together this summer, I have no intention of continuing to call you Miss Anders. And I'd like you to call me Kent."

"All right—Kent," she said haltingly.

Spotting the title of the work on his desk, Morgan let out a little gasp of pleasure. "*Last Liberty,* by Kensington T. Martin," she read almost reverently.

"Have you read it?" Kent asked.

"Yes. It was wonderful," she said. "And you're writing the screenplay based on his book!" She stared at Kent for a moment. "Why doesn't the author write it himself?" she asked.

Kent studied her before replying dryly, "He's probably too busy cranking out another best seller. The critics claim he just churns these things out effortlessly," he said crisply. "Or he could be too busy running around with all those glamorous women of his," he added with a brittle laugh.

Morgan nodded with a sigh. "Yes, I've read about his wild escapades." Then, giving him a sharp look, she added, "But don't belittle him, Kent. I happen to think he's one of the best writers I've ever read."

"I suppose you've read so many authors," he said sarcastically.

"Enough to know what I like," she retorted.

"Did you read his first novel?" Kent asked with sudden interest.

"Yes. That's how I happened to start reading all his novels as soon as they were available in the library. I couldn't wait for another book by him," she said, still gazing at the title on his desk. "I can't wait to see what you'll do with this. Will there be many changes for the movie?"

"Some changes," Kent explained. "Since some of the parts for the movie have been cast, I can put in certain mannerisms of the actors which weren't in the novel. I can tailor each part to a particular actor or actress. But the basic plot of the novel won't be changed in any way."

"Oh, that's good," she said as she sighed. "I'd hate to have you tamper with something so special." Again she ran her hand almost lovingly over the book cover. "I can't believe I'm actually going to be typing the screenplay for one of my favorite novels," she said.

"Don't get too carried away by it all," Kent said dryly. "There's nothing glamorous about our job. Now, if you'll excuse me," he said abruptly, "I'd like to get back to work. Look around the lodge and decide where you'd like to set up shop. You'll find a typewriter and office supplies stored in the back room. And Morgan," he cautioned as she started to leave, "I don't care how you spend your time here on Hidden Island, as long as you're able to do the work I've hired you to do. There's very little stimulation here. We have no radio or television or visitors, except for Old Joe. You can swim, hike, lie around in the sun. But there's no boat here. If we need anything from the mainland, I send up a signal for the ferry to stop and pick me up. There are quite a few good books on shelves in the living room. You're welcome to read them. Other than that, you'll have to create your own diversions."

Kent's words didn't disturb Morgan. Even without any news from the outside world or radio or television to entertain her, she wasn't worried about finding enough to keep her busy. Besides the mound of work already piled up on Kent's desk, Morgan knew she could fill the hours. She had never known the meaning of the word *boredom*.

After a careful study of the layout of the lodge, Morgan selected the sunny enclosed side porch for her office. It offered her a sweeping view of the island and the water beyond, and it was far enough from Kent's room to allow her to type without disturbing his work or sleep. In a small, unused bedroom, Morgan found several dusty pieces of furniture she wanted to add to her new office. After obtaining Kent's permission to use whatever she wanted, Morgan hauled a beautiful, old wicker chair and settee outside to be thoroughly scrubbed.

Ambling out on the back porch, Kent surveyed a strange scene. Morgan, dressed in a pair of faded jeans and a musty, torn, old shirt she had found in a closet of the spare room, was busily scrubbing the wicker furniture with an old scrub brush. She was so engrossed in her work, she wasn't even aware of him until he stood beside her on the grass.

"Why are you bothering with all this?" he asked.

Morgan jumped at the sound of his voice. "Oh! I

52

didn't hear you coming," she said. Sitting back on her heels to survey her handiwork, she added, "You did tell me to use whatever I wanted. I thought you wouldn't mind."

"I don't mind. But it seems to be a lot of work for just these short summer months." He frowned and added dryly, "I suppose that's the so-called nesting instinct. No matter how brief her stay, a woman just can't be content until she has made everything homey."

He was staring down at her. Suddenly dropping down beside her, he touched the sleeve of her shirt. "Where did you find this old thing?" he asked.

Morgan flinched at his touch. She looked down at her arm, unwilling to meet his eyes.

"I found it hanging in the closet of the spare room. Since it's so old and ragged, I thought you wouldn't mind if I wore it to do this work." She glanced at him. "Do you mind?"

"No," he said. "You're right. It is old and torn. It's just that I haven't seen this old shirt in years. I can hardly believe I was ever small enough to wear that."

His gaze lingered at the shirt, then his eyes moved slowly over the dark cloud of hair softly framing her face, now smudged with dirt. Her cheeks were flushed from the physical exertion of scrubbing. Her eyes, ringed by thick fringes of lashes, sparkled in the sunlight. Beads of moisture glistened on her forehead.

Abruptly he frowned and stood up. "I have so much to do," he said. "I shouldn't be wasting my time out here."

As he walked away, Morgan's eyes followed him. Gently she touched the sleeve of the old shirt. Then she frowned. Now, why in the world should it warm her to know she was wearing one of Kent's old, discarded shirts? He was practically a tyrant. But as she resumed cleaning, images of Kent as a young boy playing on this island, swimming in the cold waters of the Northumberland Strait and fishing from the dock came to her mind.

Within days Morgan's sunny little office began to reflect her personality. Besides the white wicker furniture and typing table and chair, she found several old wicker plant stands, which she set up next to her typing table. These would hold the stacks of Kent's incomplete and completed manuscript pages. She filled ancient, discarded urns with interesting dried weeds and grasses. In old-fashioned vases she collected huge bunches of wild flowers. On an old, glass-topped table she set out some of the stones and shells she collected on her daily walks about the island. In a delicate crystal vase she added to her collection of bird feathers. Each time the sun's rays touched the feathers, new iridescent hues were revealed, from glossy black to palest blue, lavender and white. Morgan reveled in the wondrous new treasures she found on the island's sandy beaches. And though he claimed all this was a waste of time, Kent grudgingly admitted that it gave his spirit a lift just to walk into Morgan's office.

The days and weeks settled into a routine of sorts. Morgan's neat and orderly life was constantly thrown off-schedule by the whims of Kent Taylor.

True to his word, Kent usually worked throughout the night, often just going to bed when Morgan awoke. Sometimes he took the time to deposit the pages he had completed on Morgan's table before turning in for the day. Other times, he would collapse into bed, leaving a mound of papers strewn about his desk and dresser. Morgan would tiptoe about his room, collecting the day's work.

It was impossible to ignore the figure spread face-down on the bed. Dressed in jeans or frayed shorts, often bare to the waist, Kent lay exhausted as she moved quietly about the room.

Sometimes Morgan allowed herself to pause and study the still figure on the bed. How did he keep up the killing pace? His body was lean and trim, like a well-developed athlete. She stared at the wide, sun-bronzed shoulders rising and falling in steady rhythm. He slept peacefully, like a child after hard play.

Kent Taylor wasn't handsome. His jaw was square, giving him a defiant expression. His blond hair, which badly needed cutting, spilled in an unruly sweep across his forehead. His neck and chin, often covered by a scraggly growth of gold hair, seemed always in need of a shave. And those eyes! Instead of being icy blue, or even green, which would have been expected, they were amber, like the dusky eyes of a cat. When he grew angry, they danced with green flecks like the points of a flame. Other times, they seemed almost colorless.

Morgan's eyes trailed to his narrow waist and his bare legs covered with a fine film of gold hair. If there were hundreds of men, immaculately groomed and tailored to perfection, Morgan knew that Kent Taylor would still command attention. There was a magnetism about the man, despite his disinterest in his appearance. But, she reminded herself, he was surly, abrupt, opinionated and the last person with whom she would have chosen to spend her summer.

Where Morgan was orderly, Kent was completely disorganized about his personal life. In his bedroom his clothes lay wherever he dropped them. There were notebooks and pencils scattered about the room. He often made himself breakfast late at night while the rest of the world slept.

But he was scrupulous about his mail. Kent had arranged for all his messages to be sent to the post office in Port Elgin. Old Joe dropped them off whenever he was passing by the island, or Kent would stop by for them when he went to the mainland for supplies. He insisted upon having Joe deliver all the mail directly into his hands.

"Even if I'm sleeping when Joe comes here," he warned Morgan, "I want him to deliver the mail directly to me. Is that completely understood?"

She nodded. Morgan didn't understand his compulsion about his correspondence, but she assumed he was just being careful not to overlook any messages from Reynolds Standish, the brilliant but demanding director.

As Kent had warned, he seemed unconcerned about his appearance or about the life that went on around him on the secluded island. It appeared that his only concern was the screenplay.

No matter how late Morgan stayed awake or awoke briefly in the night, she noticed his light burning and heard his furious pacing about the room as he worked. Within a short time she became accustomed to that sound, finding it oddly comforting in the darkness.

Having grown up in the city, Morgan was surprised at how easily she adapted to the solitude of Hidden Island. After a lifetime of automobile horns, traffic, blaring radios and people shouting, the complete silence of the island was a shocking change.

Morgan learned to listen for the musical chirp of the birds, the muted foghorn of the distant ferry laden with swarms of tourists bound for Prince Edward Island, the drone of an airplane overhead, the evening chorus of crickets. Gradually she became accustomed to the pattern of life on the island.

In the early dawn the island was shrouded in mist, which crept up in the darkness. If she managed to awaken early enough, Morgan could see the fishing fleet leaving their picturesque fishing villages and the shelter of the bays and inlets. These men daily tested their ancient skills against the sullen, defiant sea and returned home at the end of a long day with their catch of lobster, shrimp, snow crab or herring. Standing among the trees near shore, Morgan felt a thrill as she watched the huge boats passing through the swirl of mist in the strait toward the Saint Lawrence.

Early one morning, as she stood on the shore watching the fishing fleet glide silently by, Kent startled her.

"Oh!" Morgan said in a hushed tone. "What in the world are you doing up at this hour?"

"I couldn't sleep," he commented. "Too much on my mind, I suppose."

He turned and watched a lobster boat move past them, then disappear into a fog bank. "So you like to watch the fishing boats, too?"

She nodded, suddenly warmed by the thought that he shared her interest in the fleet. Kent had pulled on a heavy, white knit sweater. Morgan could see the bulge of muscle along his upper arms.

"Most of the fishermen are Acadians," he said. "Do you know much about them?"

She shook her head, not trusting her voice. He was standing too close to her. She had to tip her head back to see his face.

"The Acadians consider themselves different from the French of Quebec," Kent said. "Their ancestors came from central and western France, rather than Normandy and Brittany, like most of the Quebec French. Even their language is different. At least their dialects are very different."

"They're a very proud people," he went on. "They even have their own national anthem, the 'Ave Maris Stella,' and their own flag, a version of the French revolutionary tricolor with a gold star in the blue stripe to represent the Stella Maris, the Star of Mary."

He turned and studied her for a moment, his eyes lingering on the cloud of silken black hair, the brown eyes wide with interest. "I wish I had more time," he muttered. "You'd love some of the smaller fishing villages, where you can eat the fresh fish and lobster from the day's catch. Some of the small inns around here serve the finest seafood dinners I've ever tasted. Maybe, if our work goes well, we'll take the time for some sightseeing."

He watched the slow smile of pleasure his words had given her.

"I wish it could be today," he said, "but I just have too much yet to do." Seemingly reluctant, he turned away.

Morgan watched as Kent made his way slowly back to the lodge. That was the nicest history lesson she had ever heard. When Kent spoke about the Acadian fishermen, they seemed so much more real than anything she had ever read in a book. He made these people seem special to her. Old Joe, in his launch—an Acadian. Descendant of ancient French fishermen. Maybe that was why Kent treated him so warmly. He had respect for the traditions of these people. Morgan thought about the night she had arrived in Port Elgin, frightened, cold, alone. Both Alphonse Gagnon and Old Joe had gone out of their way to see her safely here. She recalled Joe's kind offer of a blanket and his casual dismissal of any pay for the trip across the Northumberland Strait. They were a proud and good people.

As Morgan made her way along the beach, she thought of the impatient, mysterious man she worked for. He seemed as unfathomable as the red waters off the coast of Prince Edward Island, tough and craggy as the cliffs and rocks rising out of the waters of the Saint Lawrence. But deep inside that hard shell, he harbored a warm feeling for this country and its people. Maybe there was a warmth for other things as well buried deep inside him.

The morning sun gradually burned away the mist,

leaving the island sparkling and fresh. By late afternoon Morgan usually stripped off her warm clothing in exchange for a bikini. Alone on a sun-warmed rock, she would bask for an hour or two in complete tranquility, unaware of the slow transformation taking place. Her skin became bronzed. Her thick, black hair and the dark eyelashes ringing her wide brown eyes gleamed blue-black in the brilliant sunlight. Often wearing just a pair of brief shorts and a cotton shirt casually tied about her midriff, Morgan felt free to roam the small island.

Whenever Kent awoke, usually late in the afternoon, he donned bathing trunks and jogged around the island for several miles, then ended the exercise with a long, solitary swim in the lake. Morgan tried to time her sunbathing so that she wouldn't have to be outside when Kent was there. She didn't want to intrude on his privacy. But with Kent's erratic schedule, it was inevitable that their paths would sometimes cross.

One lazy afternoon Morgan lay atop the rock she had claimed as her own. The sun and the slap of waves against the shore lulled her into a half-sleep. The tie of her bikini was undone, baring her back to the sunshine. A sudden movement startled her. Clutching the flimsy piece of fabric, she sat up and stared about her. Kent was standing in the water, his face nearly level with hers.

"I thought you were asleep," he said, studying her somberly.

"I was—until you woke me," she answered, hurriedly knotting the string around her back.

His eyes followed the movement, and Morgan looked away, blushing.

She searched her mind vainly for something to say that would fill the awkward silence.

"All this sun is turning you as brown as a berry," Kent said admiringly.

"And you look . . ." She stopped, embarrassed. She couldn't say what she was thinking—that he looked like some rugged Greek god emerging from the sea. Instead, she finished weakly, ". . . pretty healthy, too. Not like someone who spends all his time in a room struggling over the proper choice of words."

"Struggling over words!" he sputtered in mock anger. "My dear girl, I'll have you know this is a genius at work. We never struggle. The words just flow like wine from our silver tongues."

Morgan laughed aloud at his unexpected nonsense. She had never before seen Kent Taylor do or say anything silly or spontaneous. It seemed completely out of character.

Grinning, Kent added, "As long as the genius is resting his mind, why not race me to the raft out there."

Morgan turned to where he pointed and saw a small raft bobbing on the waves about a hundred yards from shore.

"All right. You're on," she called as she stood poised to dive from the rock.

Morgan was a strong swimmer, but she had no chance to beat Kent. He cut smoothly through the waves and pulled himself easily onto the raft. When

Morgan reached the raft, she clung to the rough edge, her chest heaving from the effort. Kent leaned down, extending his hands. As she offered him her hand, he lifted her from the water easily, as though she were a feather.

She felt a shock as his arms encircled her bare waist to steady her on the gently rocking raft. Her startled eyes stared into his amber cat's eyes and saw them narrow slightly as he looked down at her.

Despite the warmth of the sun, Morgan felt the prickle of gooseflesh. She shivered slightly as Kent's hands began a rhythmic circular motion on her arms and upward to her shoulders.

"Cold?" he murmured.

"No," she said too quickly. Her own voice sounded husky in her ears.

She stood, frozen to the spot, unable to move even her arms, which she still held stiffly at her sides.

"Does this feel better?" he asked, moving his hands along her shoulders. His breath felt warm across her temple, where it fanned dripping wisps of hair.

"No," she breathed, feeling her voice choke in her constricted throat.

"No?" he challenged as his mouth began to slowly descend toward hers.

His hands moved up her throat to cup her face. A jumble of emotions collided in her brain—distrust, fear, confusion.

He studied her face, seeming to read her mind. Slowly, lazily, his face descended toward hers. His lips brushed hers as gently as a flower petal, tasting, savoring their cool, velvet wetness.

Kent lifted his head, and Morgan stared, fascinated at the intensity in his eyes. He lowered his head again, his lips nibbling away her fear and distrust.

When he raised his head momentarily, he read a new emotion on her lovely face—the first stirrings of desire.

Slowly, deliberately, he lowered his head. This time, Morgan rose on tiptoe to meet his kiss. For support, she blindly reached out. With a shock, her hands found the firm, solid flesh at his waist.

As their kiss deepened, Morgan's hands slid upward along his wet skin, feeling the ripple of muscled flesh along his shoulders. Beads of water dripped from his sun-kissed hair to trickle across her upturned face. He kissed away the drops of water, causing tiny stars to explode in her brain.

Was it the urgency of his kiss or the swaying of the raft that made her world spin in dizzy circles?

Suddenly alarmed by the ease with which she had responded to him, Morgan abruptly pushed herself from his arms and stepped to the edge of the raft. She sliced into the cold water of the lake and swam the entire distance to shore without once looking back.

On shore, as she lay struggling for breath, taking great gulps of air into her aching lungs, Morgan's eyes searched the water until she made out the shape of the raft in the distance, with Kent still standing where she had left him.

Badly shaken, she walked wearily back to the lodge. As she toweled herself dry, she fretted over what had just happened. How had she allowed herself to get into that situation? Up until now, she and Kent had been able to maintain a working relationship. But it must not develop into anything else. She shivered. His experience with women was obvious from the way he had just deviously manipulated her into that whole scene. And her inexperience must be just as obvious to him by now. Kent was probably amused by her reaction. Morgan hurled the towel angrily against the wall. Now how was she going to be able to go on acting as though she weren't aware of him—as a man?

Chapter Four

The world lay in the last few moments of complete darkness before the first light of dawn. There was a silence about the island. Shrouded in tiny tufts of mist, the early pink fingers of light glimmered across the waters of the Northumberland Strait. The orange ball of the sun seemed to rise directly out of the water.

Morgan stood by the water's edge, awed—as she had been so often since her arrival here—by the spectacular beauty of each sunrise.

She had spent a sleepless night, tossing and turning in the narrow bed, hearing the furious pacing in Kent's room. In her mind she had gone over every little detail of the unexpected scene on the raft with Kent. Her response to this man, a man she didn't even like, was shocking. She tried to blame it on his obvious experience with women. He had known all the right things to do. And she had probably reacted just as he expected. Still, she was disturbed by the deep feelings his simple touch had aroused in her. If she really didn't like him, how could she have melted so willingly in his arms?

All night, Morgan had been unable to shake the vision of Kent Taylor, his lean, athletic body tanned by the sun and glistening with silvery droplets of water. Kent had become magnified in her mind—the forbidden fruit. And each time she thought about his lips, moist and urgent on hers, she tingled with a new awareness of budding desire. His image would not be dispelled. Instead of fading as the night faded, the apparition of Kent grew stronger, filling her mind, leaving her no room for other thoughts.

Finally, resigned to the fact that sleep would not be forthcoming, she dressed and slipped silently out the door to watch the dawn.

Even the waves lapping the shore were muted in the early morning. An occasional gull shrieked, then disappeared with its breakfast of fish. Shivering in the damp mist, Morgan turned toward the lodge, then stopped abruptly. Kent was walking down the steps in her direction.

His feet were bare. In his typical collection of rumpled clothes, his faded jeans and wrinkled plaid cotton shirt looked as though they had been slept in for a week. Even from this distance, she could see that his hair was tousled.

His eyes skimmed over her quickly, noting the fatigue about her eyes, a certain tenseness at the corners of her mouth.

"I thought it was time I did the cooking," he said

with studied casualness. "Come on in. I've made breakfast."

Morgan groaned inwardly, recalling her first experience with his cooking. But at least he wasn't deliberately avoiding her. She had feared he might shun her after yesterday's awkward encounter.

"I think I'll just have coffee and toast and get to my typewriter," she said, groping for an excuse to avoid eating.

"There won't be much to type," he said quietly. "I didn't get too much accomplished last night."

She detected a strange, almost halting quality to his brisk words. Was it regret, apology? Or just her imagination? They walked back to the lodge, each lost in private thoughts.

It was a terrible breakfast in every way. The eggs had been fried into hard globs. As usual, the toast was burned. Kent even had squeezed fresh orange juice and had allowed the seeds to fall into the glass. Kent and Morgan ate their entire meal in strained silence. As Morgan jabbed her spoon down in the juice to remove yet another seed, she chanced a glance at Kent's face.

He was watching her. "Surprised?" he asked, indicating the breakfast he had prepared.

"Yes." She frowned, then suddenly burst out laughing, releasing all her pent-up tension. At his puzzled frown, she added, "Yes, I am surprised you would attempt another breakfast. No, I'm not surprised at how awful all this tastes."

Seeing his mock wounded expression, she added, "Kent, I hope you write screenplays better than you cook."

He leaned back, relieved to see the laughter back in her eyes. "So you don't appreciate my surprise? All right, Miss Anders, then you get to do the dishes."

"Gladly." She chuckled. "It will give me a chance to work off the lump that has settled in my stomach."

He watched her as she picked up a dishtowel and began carrying dishes to the sink. He leaned back with a cup of weak coffee and smiled contentedly. She seemed to be her cheerful self again.

"I suddenly feel like working," he said eagerly. "I'll see you later."

For the next several hours Morgan was glad to once again hear the sounds of Kent's restless pacing. As he had admitted, his long night had produced little work for her to type.

In the late afternoon Joe came to the island with Kent's mail. Morgan lay on the white sandy beach enjoying the sun when she heard the throb of engines that signaled Joe's launch. She hurried to the lodge to get some letters she had written. Joe would deliver them to the post office in Port Elgin for her.

As she came out of her room, Kent was just heading down to the dock. He turned at her footsteps, a lazy, relaxed smile softening the tired lines about his mouth.

"I have some mail. I thought Joe could drop it at the post office for me," she said.

"I'll take it," Kent said, holding out his hand. "I'm just going down to the dock now."

As Morgan handed him the letters, his eye fell on the top envelope.

"What is this?" he demanded fiercely. The smile had frozen, to be replaced instantly by a blaze of hot anger.

Morgan was startled by his tone. Defensively, she said, "What does it look like? It's a letter to a friend."

"A friend who just happens to work for the New York *Press?*" He towered over her, his fist clenched tightly at his side.

"Yes." She paused. "He works in the circulation department. Why?" Morgan was aware of a barely contained fury in his manner.

Within seconds, Kent's expression became closed and hard. But the green points of flame leaped in his eyes, and a tiny pulse worked at the base of his tightly clenched jaw. His sudden rage carefully in check, he turned away from Morgan stiffly. His body seemed as tightly coiled as a spring.

Without another word, Kent made his way to the dock. Standing at the back door, Morgan watched him accept his mail and messages from Joe and hand him a packet of mail. He spent a few minutes in conversation with Joe, then turned. As he made his way back across the sweep of weeds and wild-flower strewn ground, he glanced at her figure in the doorway, then looked away. He entered, swept past her stiffly, and without a word, made his way to his room.

Morgan was so confused she couldn't even begin to sort out what had happened. One minute Kent was happily accepting her mail, and the next he was enraged. What in the world had she said or done to make him so furious? His anger seemed to be directed toward her letter. But that was ridiculous. Kent couldn't possibly be jealous that she was writing to a friend, even if he assumed, wrongly, that it was a boyfriend. Her personal life was none of his business. And Kent didn't strike Morgan as the sort of man who would be petty and insecure. And if he disapproved of the New York *Press,* that was his own problem. None of this made any sense to her.

In the days that followed, Kent threw himself into a frenzy of work, to Morgan's great relief. There was no better way for the two to avoid contact with each other than to have Kent work in the seclusion of his room while Morgan typed in her small office or spent long hours outside, where there was little chance of running into him.

Several times he wrote frantically through the night, slept for a few hours, then started in again, like someone possessed. Near the end of the week he worked around the clock, not stopping to eat or sleep. Like a man driven, his mood became agitated and surly. The pile of neatly typed pages was once again turned into a jumble of scribbled, crumpled papers. And where Morgan was concerned, Kent's temper seemed at the breaking point. He criticized her work until she was near tears.

"Morgan!" he shouted one day. "Where are you?"

Morgan, toweling herself after a swim, jerked her head up and looked toward the sound of the hostile voice.

"I'm out here," she called.

"Well, get in here!" he commanded.

Gritting her teeth, Morgan deliberately took her

time, tying the beach towel around her wet bathing suit, neatly tucking the ends into the front of her suit. She bent and pulled on a pair of sandals, then straightened and walked slowly toward the lodge, steeling herself for another verbal assault.

Kent was standing by her typing table. Strewn about the floor were dozens of papers from the wastebasket. Kent's arms were held stiffly at his sides with both fists clenching crumpled papers. Seeing her, his eyes blazed.

"Where is page four hundred twenty-two?" he demanded.

"Forgive me if I don't come up with it immediately," she said sarcastically.

"Look here," he said, pointing to the manuscript on her table. "This is page four hundred twenty-one. Here is page four hundred twenty-three. So where is the missing page?"

"I probably just numbered them wrong," she said impatiently.

"No. I checked. There's an entire scene missing here. A key scene. It was a tender moment between the man and woman. I remember writing it," he snapped.

"Really!" she retorted. "I wouldn't expect you to know how to write a tender scene. Are you sure it wasn't a fight scene instead?"

His head shot up, and he regarded her coldly. "The woman in this movie is a real woman," he hissed through his teeth. "Warm and giving and loving."

"Why you . . ." In her fury, Morgan's hand shot out automatically.

71

Kent caught it before she could strike his face. He pulled her toward him with such force, she collided against the granite wall of his chest.

She found herself staring into his smoldering eyes. Amber flames of fire sparked in the tawny haze. Her thick, dark eyelashes swept down to hide her confusion. The papers dropped from his other hand, and Kent caught her chin in a tight grip and forced her to look up at him.

Her breath caught in her throat, then forced its way out in a deep, shuddering sigh. He felt the slight tremor of her body, and a wave of warring emotions crossed his face. Morgan could only stare in fascination as he held her against him, slowly, deliberately, bringing his hands around to pin her tightly against his hard, lean body.

In one last, desperate bid for sanity, she whispered, "Don't, Kent."

He seemed drawn to her against his own will. The words were stilled by the force of his lips on hers. With her breath strangling in her throat, she pushed ineffectively against him. This only reinforced his determination. His hands slid seductively along her back, and one hand suddenly caught at the tangles of silken hair, pulling her head back and molding her even tighter against him.

Slowly, languorously, her hands moved up to grip his shoulders for support. A tiny flame began curling in the pit of her stomach. Heated anger suddenly burned into simmering desire.

Abruptly, Kent dropped his hands. She felt suddenly cold and empty. Staring up into his face, her breath still ragged and painful, she swayed toward him. He caught her roughly by the shoulders and stared down at her lips, still moist and swollen from his kiss.

Contemptuously, he dropped his hands, as though the very touch of her disturbed him.

Turning on his heel, he said savagely, "I want that page on my desk. Don't take your sweet time searching for it. I want it within the next five minutes." With that, he strode from the room.

Morgan stood, rooted to the spot, without moving a muscle, staring at his retreating back. The effect his touch had on her was frightening. Morgan knew she couldn't possibly allow herself to get involved with Kent Taylor. In the end, she would get hurt. Common sense told her to keep her distance from him no matter what harsh words he hurled at her or how persuasive his kisses.

Gritting her teeth, Morgan was stung by what he had implied. According to Kent Taylor, a woman who fell willingly into a man's arms and allowed herself to be carried along by the tide of passion was warm and giving and loving. A kind of earth mother. But if a woman had a sense of responsibility about herself, had a sense of what she wanted out of life, wasn't willing to settle for just the satisfaction of the moment, she was—frigid!

With more vengeance than the situation required, Morgan began scanning every paper in her room. After a thorough search of her cluttered wastebasket, Morgan found the missing page. With the beach towel still wrapped around her damp bathing suit, she walked into his room, wordlessly handed him the paper and strode stiffly away.

His eyes burned into her rigid back.

A few days later, the scene was nearly repeated.

It was evening. Morgan, dressed in a sweater and jeans, was in the kitchen making herself a cup of tea. Kent stormed into the room like a wounded bull, complete with stomping feet and flaring nostrils.

"Just when did you become a screenwriter, Miss Anders?" he demanded.

She whirled from the stove. "What?"

"By whose authority did you change my words?" he said.

"I type exactly what you write and nothing more," she defended herself.

"Is that so?" he asked sarcastically, dropping a page on the kitchen table and scowling at her. "Then would you explain this, please."

He produced his handwritten page and set it beside her typewritten page.

Morgan moved to his side, suddenly so aware of him that her skin tingled, and bent to study the two papers. She straightened and faced him, forcing herself to remain calm. She would not give him the satisfaction of showing him how his very presence beside her could destroy her composure.

"All right. I did pick up the wrong words here," she admitted. "But you can certainly understand how it happened. Take a look at this scribble. I defy anyone to decipher this mess."

"But you do admit changing my words?" he insisted.

"Yes. I typed the wrong words. But it wasn't done deliberately. If you weren't so busy being so—so arrogant," she sputtered, "you'd have seen for yourself how it happened."

She turned from him in a rage, feeling close to tears. "All you had to do was make the corrections and set the paper on my typing table. I would have returned it to you with the proper words. But no!" she nearly shouted. "You enjoy lording it over me with your egotistical display of intelligence!"

Seeing the shocked look on his face, Morgan headed for the kitchen door. Over her shoulder, she called defiantly, "You're never civil to me anymore. I'm so sick and tired of your temper tantrums."

In the doorway she was spun around by the force of his hands. Jolted, she stared into his narrowed, tawny eyes. He moved menacingly nearer.

In almost a whisper he said, "I can't afford to be civil to you, Morgan Anders. I might find myself caught in your web."

"Web?" she repeated, confused.

He towered over her, his hands still roughly holding her shoulders. His face was so close to hers, she could feel his breath feather her hair as he sought to control his anger.

Softly, he said, "Either you are the most innocent woman I have ever met, or you are one of the world's greatest actresses."

His hands were pressing into her flesh, causing her to wince. His eyes fixed on her lips, seemingly unaware of the pain his grip was causing.

Her eyes grew round. The black pupils seemed to glow in the dim light.

Against his will, he drew her into the circle of his arms, pressing his lips against her temple. "Morgan," he murmured against her hair. "Do you know what you're doing to . . ."

His lips moved along her forehead, raining kisses on her eyes, her cheeks, her throat. He kissed every part of her face and neck, except her lips. Morgan heard breathy, little sighs of pleasure and realized they were her own. Slowly, her hands crawled along his back, feeling the firm flesh through the thin fabric of his shirt. She needed to cling to his strength.

Suddenly, she could no longer wait for his lips to find hers. With a little moan, she lifted her lips to seek his. Hungrily, their lips came together in a lingering kiss. Breathless, Morgan sighed, then tilted her head for yet another of his drugging kisses. Kent bent his head to her.

Shivers of delight sent tremors through her. His kiss became more urgent. His hands pressed against her hips, molding her to his lean, hard frame. She could feel the strength of his thighs against her own.

A moment later he moved a step away from her. She felt suddenly cold. She shivered and moved toward him.

With great tenderness, he caught her face in both his hands and stared down at her. There was a light in his eyes that she had never seen before. His look burned over her face, as if to memorize every line and curve. Very gently, he brushed her lips with his, then dropped his hands suddenly. His face changed, the features growing harsher, and he strode away.

The following morning Kent's feverish work stopped abruptly. Morgan found him sprawled, face-down, on a sofa in the living room. It was nearly dawn, and the coals in the fireplace were still warm. Shivering in the early morning chill, she stared at Kent's still form, clad only in a pair of ragged shorts, one bare foot hanging over the end of the sofa arm. She tiptoed away, relieved that he was finally asleep. Sometimes she found herself worrying about his crazy work habits. It just didn't seem healthy to go for such long hours, and sometimes days, without sleep. But, she reminded herself time and again, he was a grown man, capable of running his own life. If he wanted to ruin his health and his nerves, that was his business. He meant nothing more to her than a paycheck, she told herself as she draped a blanket over his sleeping form.

Chapter Five

Without warning, Kent announced that they were going to the mainland for the day.

"I think we've both earned a day off," he said simply as he found Morgan in the kitchen making early morning coffee.

"Oh, I'd love it." She sighed. "You mean the whole day?" Her face glowed with pleasure.

"Why not? I need to go to the post office and store, anyway," he said blandly. He watched the swift change of emotions mirrored in her expressive face.

"Oh." She felt suddenly deflated. She should have known Kent wouldn't suggest a day off just for fun.

"But after I take care of my business, we can explore the countryside a bit," he added.

Her smile returned. "Oh, how wonderful." She

beamed. "I've been dying to see New Brunswick, and Prince Edward Island, and . . ."

"Wait a minute!" Kent interrupted gruffly. "I said the day off. Not the month. I don't think we're going to get to see much of the country in one day, Morgan."

She laughed in delight. "A day is better than nothing. I'll be ready in a little while." She danced down the hall toward her room.

Dressed in a pale yellow sundress for the warmth of the late afternoon and a matching yellow sweater for the coolness of the morning and the breezy ride on the ferry, Morgan brushed her thick, dark hair until it gleamed. She pulled on a comfortable pair of rope-soled espadrilles for the trek through the town. Into a yellow shoulder bag she stowed a hairbrush, lipstick, perfume and wallet. With another quick check in the mirror above her dresser, Morgan was ready for a day on the mainland.

Kent was standing on the porch, watching the horizon for the ferry. As he turned, Morgan noted his dark brown slacks and beige shirt, accenting the cool blond hair and deep tan of his chest and arms.

His eyes lingered on her as he said, "You look like the wild daisy that grows here on the island—black-eyed Susan."

While she felt herself blushing down to her toes, he suddenly grabbed her hand, and they descended the steps. Morgan felt as giddy as any girl on her first date.

A whole day away from the typewriter and the

confines of their tiny island. It seemed like an adventure. They both began to run as the foghorn sounded from the approaching ferry.

On deck, they stood at the railing and watched as Hidden Island fell away into the distance. Gulls soared above, gliding on currents of air, then dipping suddenly to snatch their meal from the water.

They stood apart at the railing, each pretending to be deeply absorbed by the antics of the gulls. But Morgan was keenly aware of the exact moment when Kent's eyes moved to study her. She forced herself to remain at the railing, her gaze studiously fastened on the churning foam far below.

Morgan's dark hair fanned out in the stiff breeze. Kent, moving to stand beside her, reached out and smoothed a silken strand.

"Aren't you worried about the wind ruining your hairstyle?" he asked.

She laughed. "What hairstyle? All I do is brush out the tangles and let it curl as it pleases."

"I know women who would have their hair lacquered and sprayed into place and covered with a scarf so it wouldn't get mussed," he said grimly.

The look he gave her made her heart skip several beats before settling back to its natural rhythm. A tremor ran through her, and Kent removed his windbreaker and wrapped it about her shoulders.

"This ride is always windy," he muttered thickly, his voice so near her ear that another tremor shot through her slender body.

"Come on," he ordered, wrapping his arms protectively about her to ward off the breeze. "Let's stand in the sun on the forward deck."

Morgan allowed him to lead her, savoring the strange, unfamiliar delight of feeling protected.

The ride ended quickly, with the deafening blast of the ferry's horn announcing their arrival at the mainland. With great commotion, the ferry docked and the cars and people went about their ritual of disembarking. Kent caught Morgan's hand and led her down the gangplank.

As they strolled along the main street of Port Elgin, Morgan said, "When I was a little girl, Gramps took me to a county fair in a small town in upstate New York. This town reminds me of it. The same small grocery store and church with the cemetery beside it. The same small-town feeling. I love it. I feel today like I did that day at the fair. Did you ever go to a county fair?" she asked.

"No. But you make it sound like fun." Then he smiled, and his voice softened. "As soon as I finish my errands, let's get a good breakfast."

"Are we going to the diner?" she asked.

"No, there's a place up the coast I think you'll like," he replied.

"Up the coast. How will we get there?" she protested.

"I keep a jeep at the gas station," Kent said smugly. "Just in case I have a day like today and want to get away."

Morgan frowned. Kent was certainly secretive. In all the time she had been here, this was the first she heard about his owning a vehicle. After stopping at the small grocery store with a supply list, they checked into the post office for Kent's mail and phone messages.

"Morgan, while I pick up the mail, dial this number for me," Kent said.

Glancing at the card he handed her, Morgan's eyes grew wide. "Reynolds Standish?" she asked in awe.

"Yes. It may take a few minutes to get through to California. Just tell him you're my secretary and ask him to hold for my call."

Kent strode away, leaving Morgan to handle the long-distance operator. When she finally heard the director's voice, Morgan smiled to herself. Imagine talking to a famous director in Hollywood! Within minutes, Kent was there to complete the call.

They walked to the gas station. Alphonse Gagnon was nowhere in sight. A young man was pumping gas. Probably the young man from town who helped out as a mechanic, Morgan thought.

The stranger smiled a greeting to Kent and indicated the keys that were hanging on a nail inside the station. From behind the building, Kent drove a small, open jeep. Morgan climbed into the passenger side, and they took off in a cloud of dust. Clinging tightly to the door, Morgan laughed in delight as they rounded a curve and followed the shoreline out of town.

The twisting, narrow road wound through miles of rich farmland. Morgan leaned back and enjoyed the fresh breeze, the scent of newly mown hay, the unfamiliar sweet, dank smell of ploughed earth.

As the road merged with a two-lane paved highway, they drove past rows of comfortable old houses with beautifully manicured lawns, carefully tended gardens and brilliant strips of flower beds brimming with every imaginable color.

The town that lay beyond was larger than Port Elgin, with a modern shopping mall and scores of restaurants and shops. Kent parked, and catching her hand in his, they walked along until they came to a sidewalk cafe with brightly striped awnings and tables and chairs in candy-striped colors set up outdoors with bright umbrellas for shade. It was the perfect place to enjoy breakfast and watch the parade of pedestrians passing by.

After a huge breakfast of ham, eggs, pancakes and strong, black coffee, topped off with delicate, freshly baked pastries, they left the sidewalk cafe to browse the fascinating shops that lined both sides of the wide boulevard.

In an antique shop Kent bought a heavy brass cricket doorstop for the lodge. Morgan commented that there were already enough of the live variety of crickets chirping in the early morning and late evening hours. They didn't need more. Laughing, Kent told the salesgirl to wrap it up.

In a china shop specializing in English bone china, Kent found a fine, translucent white cup and saucer with a yellow daisy pattern.

Holding it up, he called, "Guess who this reminds me of?"

The salesclerk looked from one to the other, puzzled by their shared laughter.

"Would you like it, sir?" she asked.

"Yes," he said, winking at Morgan.

Her heart stopped for a moment, and she turned away to hide her emotions.

Next, they entered an interesting-looking shop that carried every conceivable kind of lace. Morgan exclaimed over exquisite lace handkerchiefs and tablecloths. As they passed a bridal display Kent impulsively reached out and placed an elegant bridal veil on Morgan's head. The delicate white lace lay on her thick, black hair and framed her face, giving her an ethereal appearance.

Kent caught her chin and studied her. "Morgan, you're breathtaking. Like a madonna," he whispered.

She felt the heat rush to her face, flooding her cheeks. To hide her embarrassment at his compliment, she turned away and returned the veil to the display case.

Kent led Morgan through a dusty old book shop, where volumes of Shakespeare resided beside old French cookbooks. They spent hours studying the titles of books, laughing together at some of the volumes they found. Morgan bought two modern novels she had been intending to read, and Kent picked up a book of verse. With their purchases tucked under their arms, they finally tore themselves away from the fascinating old shop and strolled further along the street.

"Are you enjoying yourself?" Kent asked.

Swinging along by his side, Morgan enthused, "Oh yes, Kent. I love this town."

"I thought you'd like it. Through the years, whenever I got the chance, which wasn't often, I've tried to spend some time here."

Back in the jeep, they soon left the town and

its lovely houses far behind. The coastline now became rocky and heavily forested, resembling the posters Morgan had seen of the Canadian wilderness.

Turning to Kent, she said, laughing, "I fully expect any minute now to see a Mountie riding out of the woods."

Kent joined the laughter. "It does look that way, doesn't it."

Morgan enjoyed the ride in complete relaxation. There was no tension between them. This seemed to be a special day, to be hugged to her heart like an unexpected gift. She leaned back and watched Kent skillfully maneuver the jeep around curves. If only he could always be this way—laughing, teasing, unmindful of the deadline for the manuscript. He seemed like another person. Morgan sighed in bliss and stole a glance at Kent's profile. He turned, and catching her look, returned her smile. Her heart soared.

Kent turned the wheel sharply, and the jeep veered off the main road onto a narrow, rutted path. For nearly an hour they drove through thickly forested passages following a rough trail that at times seemed to disappear entirely, then reappeared around a bend or across a ravine. The little jeep bounced across deep ruts and shallow streams until, suddenly, they emerged in brilliant sunlight along a white sandy shore. They had left the town behind and had entered one of the tiny coves Morgan had viewed from the deck of the ferry.

Grinning happily, Kent switched off the ignition and bent to remove his shoes.

"What are you doing?" Morgan asked.

"Taking off my shoes. Come on. We'll walk along the shore."

Morgan removed her espadrilles and stepped onto sun-warmed sand. With his feet bare and his pants rolled to his knees, Kent followed. As they made their way slowly along the shore, foamy waves rolled gently over their feet, occasionally sending up a spray of water to cool them.

Kent picked up a handful of stones and skimmed each one across the water, watching as they skittered, then sank with a quiet plop, sending out ripples that widened with each circle.

Each time Morgan saw an odd-shaped shell or stone, she bent and picked it up. When her hands could hold no more, Kent took them from her and stuffed them in his pockets.

They walked along nearly a mile of deserted beach, savoring the gentle bird songs and the rhythmic splash of the waves. Finally, all past tensions dissolved, and feeling completely at ease in each other's company, they turned and retraced their steps toward the jeep. Kent dropped his arm casually across her shoulders. Morgan's arm encircled his waist without a trace of self-consciousness.

As they dusted the sand from their feet, Morgan said, "Wasn't it nice of everyone to leave this little piece of land alone for us to enjoy?"

Laughing, Kent nodded.

When he switched on the engine of the jeep, Morgan asked, "Are we heading for home now?"

"Not just yet," he replied. "I thought we'd drive

up the coast farther for dinner. There's a little inn I think you'll like."

Back on the main highway, the road climbed steadily for nearly an hour. As they rounded a curve, Morgan caught her breath. In the woods to their right, nearly hidden from the road, stood an ancient-looking hotel. As they drove along the narrow path that led to the front entrance, Morgan stared in wonder. It looked like an old French castle, complete with towers and turrets. Wild flowers grew in profusion in the shade of the towering evergreens that surrounded the stone building.

Kent parked the jeep and helped Morgan to the ground. Still holding hands, they walked to the huge, wooden door intricately carved and flanked by tall, stained-glass windows. An elderly man in formal attire greeted them.

"Mr. Taylor? Good evening, sir. We've been expecting you. Will you follow me, please."

As they followed the man through a dim, high-ceilinged foyer, Morgan gave Kent a questioning glance.

He smiled and whispered, "They only prepare dinner if you phone ahead. As you can see, there are very few patrons."

They entered a cozy, wood-paneled room. It was a private dining room. They were the only people here. A round table, set with an antique lace cloth and elegant crystal and silver, stood before a crackling fire. The wood flooring, gleaming with the patina of age, and the huge stone hearth gave the room a glowing warmth.

Kent led Morgan to a window to gaze on the sloping lawns and the vineyards beyond. Wooden benches, like church pews, were set up in rose-covered arbors. A flock of doves hopped about a cobblestone-paved patio where grain had been scattered for their dinner. In the distance stood an ancient stable with a thatched roof.

Morgan sighed as she looked up at Kent. "It's like something from another time. Oh, Kent, it's beautiful."

He held her chair at the table set for two, and the old man returned with a bottle of red wine. He offered Kent a sample. Kent sipped and nodded, and the old man poured some into each of their glasses, then silently left the room.

"They make their own wine here," Kent said. "I think you'll like it."

The wine was light and delicious. Morgan wasn't accustomed to drinking wine, but she was thoroughly enjoying the experience.

Without a word, the waiter continued to enter the room with course after course. Morgan was mystified.

"Did you order all this ahead of time, Kent?" she whispered as the old man slipped silently from the room.

Kent smiled. "I only had to phone and tell them we were coming. They cook whatever they please. That's the way it's done here."

The waiter placed before them delicate pastries, fluted like sea shells, filled with lightly seasoned seafood and topped with a delicate cream sauce.

This was followed by a salad of fresh spinach with bits of chopped egg and bacon and tossed with a tangy dressing.

Silently, the waiter poured more wine, then brought poached salmon in white wine and tiny whole potatoes in a light sauce with pearl onions.

While they savored their dinner, Kent drew out Morgan's memories of her early years.

"You mentioned a grandfather, Morgan," Kent said. "What about your parents?"

"My mother died when I was five. A year later my father died, also. I went to live with Gramps. He was determined to teach me to make it on my own."

Morgan stared at the flames leaping in the fireplace. Her eyes misted. "Sometimes I resented being pushed so much by my grandfather. He was so gruff with me. But I realize now that he knew all along that I would be left alone. And he saw it as his duty to teach me independence. Even if he had to be hard on me." She smiled brightly. "And he did love me. With Gramps, everything in life was an adventure."

"Is that how you've managed to tolerate the sameness of life on the island this summer?" Kent asked. "Have you made it a kind of adventure?"

"Oh yes," Morgan said with enthusiasm. Then she flushed as she realized Kent was teasing her.

He leaned back and regarded her warmly. "You really mean it, don't you?" he asked softly.

"Yes. It really is an adventure for me. After a lifetime in the city, the island is so different." She stared down at her hands for a moment as if to sort out her words before continuing. "All my life I've been rushing to stay on schedule. There was school, of course, and since I was fifteen, there was always a job after school. It seems sometimes that I've always had to jump up for alarm clocks and bells. At the academy, where I work, there are bells between every class. And in the evening, after work, there are the college classes." She laughed before adding, "I definitely do not miss having an alarm clock this summer."

"But you don't feel—lonely or trapped on Hidden Island?" Kent persisted.

"Lonely or trapped?" Morgan shook her head emphatically. "Kent, except for Gramps, I've been alone most of my life. Even in a bustling place like New York, or maybe especially in New York, a person can be very much alone. But that isn't the same as feeling lonely. There is something pleasant about the solitude here. I'm learning so much about the rhythm of life here. I feel in touch with myself, too. I've begun to think that when I go back to the city, I'll know a little more about myself. This job has given me a chance to stand apart and explore my thoughts without the clamor and confusion of everyday living."

Morgan shook her head again, causing the thick cloud of hair to settle softly against her cheeks and shoulders. Her eyes gleamed with pleasure. "I love the solitude of your island. I haven't once felt lonely. And I'm not alone. You're there, too."

Kent leaned his arms on the table and studied her face. "Sometimes, when I'm working, I see you out walking, stooping to pick up all the crazy things you collect, and I wonder what goes through your mind."

Morgan smiled shyly. "I love those solitary walks. I've found so many treasures." Laughing, she added, "Or, as you call them, those crazy things I collect."

As Kent joined her laughter, she said softly, "You'll never know how much this summer has meant to me. I've always loved to get away to the country for the summer. In the past few summers, at Wanaway Camp, I've always had all those little boys around." She chuckled. "If you've ever been around a dozen little boys at a summer camp, you know that there is no such thing as solitude. Sometimes, they treated me like a mother, bringing me all their problems. At other times, because I'm young enough to be like an older sister, they teased me, and even on occasion tossed me in the lake." She made a face. "Once, they tossed me in the lake in my pajamas in the middle of the night!"

Kent laughed at the wry expression on her face. "Yes," he said. "I think that would prove great sport for little boys away at camp."

"But this has been a very different kind of experience," she said. "There's been time for just me. Oh, there's the typing for you, of course. I don't mean that I don't give my attention to your work. But there's no pressure to get up at a certain time or keep my old car going for another hundred miles or so. It's been like a vacation. A working vacation."

As they finished their dinner, Kent indicated the inn and the cozy room. "How do you like my surprise?" he asked.

"Oh, Kent. It's lovely," she said. Morgan's cheeks were flushed, whether from the wine, the glow of the fire or the excitement of the day she couldn't tell.

Kent stared at her eyes dancing in the firelight. "You're lovely, too," he said as he caught her hand resting on the tabletop and ran his fingertips across her wrist.

Startled, she caught back her hand and gripped her hands together tightly in her lap self-consciously.

Kent saw the betraying blush color her cheeks. "Morgan, you are a wonder," he whispered.

At that moment the waiter appeared with whole strawberries in mounds of freshly whipped cream. Morgan was grateful for his interruption. Her heart was pounding so loudly in her chest, she was afraid Kent could hear it.

After dessert, Kent sipped an after-dinner brandy while Morgan finished her coffee. The sun had already set, and tiny lights twinkled in the branches of the trees outside their window.

As they walked slowly to the jeep parked in the now-darkened courtyard, Kent said, "I'm sorry there wasn't a county fair around her. I couldn't give you cotton candy or caramel apples today. This was the best I could do."

She turned to him, beaming with pleasure. "I've already had cotton candy and caramel apples. But I've never been to a French castle before. Or drank wine from crystal goblets. It was all so wonderful. I'll never forget it." Or you, she thought as she climbed in the jeep beside him.

On the long drive back to Port Elgin, Morgan

broke the silence. "You never talk about yourself, Kent." She studied his craggy profile in the dark. "Do you have any sisters or brothers?"

"No," he said wearily. "No sisters or brothers. My father is dead. My mother has a place in Palm Springs." The words were spoken flatly.

As she opened her mouth to ask another question, he effectively silenced her by saying abruptly, "I don't like talking about myself."

She would not be sidetracked by his tactics. After a lengthy pause, she insisted, "What do you do when you're not writing screenplays?"

"I write other things," he said dryly.

"Oh! What have you written?" she asked eagerly.

"Nothing you'd be interested in," he said curtly.

Kent parked the jeep at the gas station. "We've missed the last ferry. I'll phone Old Joe for the launch," he said.

After his phone call, they walked slowly toward the wharf and stood on the pier to watch the play of lights from passing boats on the water.

Like a tenacious puppy, Morgan wouldn't let go of her desire to learn more about this mysterious man.

"You seem so annoyed by my questions, Kent," she persisted.

"You don't need to know about my personal life in order to do a good job," he snapped. "Since when does a secretary get a personal profile of her employer?"

He heard the tiny, choked gasp of pain his words had inflicted. Kent turned and studied her for a moment in the darkness. Then, with a slow intake of breath, he said, "How old are you, Morgan? Twenty?"

She nodded.

"And I'm almost twice your age," he said. "Listen, Morgan. I've learned to live with a lot of the realities of life. Some people get some perverse pleasure out of learning all they can about someone else and then twisting all the facts to make that person sound ugly and vicious. It's happened to me in the past. I'm sure it will happen again in the future. It's just a fact of life."

He paused, and Morgan watched the tiny flame as Kent touched a match to a thin cigar. The tip of the cigar glowed red-hot in the darkness. A cloud of rich smoke curled around them.

"You may call that cynical," he said. "I call it being realistic. If you don't know anything about me, you can't be coerced into sharing information about me that could be—misconstrued. So back off, Morgan. I prefer it this way."

As she began to protest, he placed his fingers over her mouth to silence her. "Let it go, Morgan. I'd hate to read something like 'My Summer with Kent Taylor' or 'I Spent My Summer in the Arms of Kent Taylor.'"

Morgan backed up, her hands on her hips, furious at his cool description of the shocking betrayal he anticipated.

"That's disgusting! How can you even suggest such a thing?"

As she turned away, he caught her arm and forced her to face him. "Oh, don't act so outraged. It happens all the time. If someone offered you so much money your head swam just thinking about it, you could justify anything by claiming that you needed the money to survive."

He removed his hand from her arm, and Morgan found herself trembling in the darkness.

"Now don't say you weren't warned in advance," he muttered. "And don't punish yourself by feeling guilty. It happens all the time. I'm getting used to it. It doesn't even matter anymore. I've read so much of that kind of publicity about myself, I'm immune to it."

"Well, I've never read about you," she said angrily. After all, who would care to read about a struggling, unknown screenwriter? Her voice shook, whether from anger or from the effects of his touch, she wasn't sure.

The loud vibrations of the launch engines drowned out anything more they had to say. As Old Joe smiled, Kent stepped aboard the launch and helped Morgan aboard. They settled themselves on the wide seat, and Morgan pulled her sweater tightly about herself to ward off the wind. A few moments later the launch slowly moved through the shallows. When they reached deep water, the engines throbbed as they picked up speed. As the boat danced roughly off the waves, Morgan held on to the side and once again felt her nerves protest the bone-crushing movement of the boat. The wind whipped her hair about wildly. She closed her eyes and held on, hoping the ride would soon end. Suddenly Kent tossed the cigar to the wind, and she felt his strong arms wrap themselves around her. Leaning toward him, she buried her face in his neck and allowed her taut muscles to relax. With his arms around her, she suddenly wished the wild boat ride would never end and she could stay locked in the safety of Kent's strong arms forever.

At the dock Kent thanked Joe and gently helped Morgan from the boat. He guided her through the darkness toward the lodge, which loomed up before them.

Walking up the wide steps, he said, "I'll start a fire. You're shivering."

Morgan knew this should be the time for her to leave and allow Kent to start on his work. But she was reluctant to end their special day. While Kent built a fire in the fireplace, she stood watching him, hugging her arms about her shoulders. She felt a trembling in her limbs, but she was certain it wasn't from the cold. She wanted him to hold her. Yet, she was afraid. The effect he had on her emotions was frightening.

Kent stood, watching the flames, then turned and saw her standing there, her arms drawn tightly about her, a frightened, luminous look in her wide, brown eyes. She looked like a terrified deer about to bolt through the forest.

His features softened, a smile crinkling the corners of his eyes. As he crossed the room toward her, he chuckled. "Don't worry, Morgan. I know I have a temper, but I don't bite."

She smiled self-consciously, and her eyelashes dropped down like brown velvet to veil her eyes. She jumped nervously at his touch.

"How did you like your day off?" he asked quietly, feeling her pulse quicken.

"It's been a lovely day," she sighed.

His eyes narrowed, watching her.

"Well, I'll let you get to work now," she said awkwardly.

His hand on her arm stopped her. "Morgan," he murmured.

The name was spoken so tenderly, her heart thudded against her ribs.

"Good night, Kent," she said, feeling her voice catch in her throat.

"Stay with me."

She froze. What was he saying?

"It—it's been a long day. I'm tired," she lied. She was so keyed up, she knew she would never get to sleep tonight. She felt a burning sensation on her arm where his hand rested. Her heart was pounding so painfully, she was afraid it would leap from her throat.

His hands caught her shoulders, urging her to stay.

A tremor of alarm ran through her. They still had so much time to be together, alone, on this island.

She jerked herself free of his touch. "No, Kent. I'm really tired. Good night."

At her door, a steel grip caught and twisted her around. His tawny eyes, blazing with emotion, held her.

"Is it too much to ask you to stay up with me awhile?" His hands dug into the flesh of her shoulders, causing her to wince.

He didn't know what he was asking of her. It

would be impossible for her to be near him while she felt this overwrought. His simple touch was tilting her world upside down.

"Yes." She was unwilling to show him how she really felt. "Yes. It is too much to ask. I'm on my own time, now. I'll spend it as I please."

As she abruptly turned her head away, his hand dug into the thick tangles of her hair, pulling her head toward him, forcing it back. Her eyes were round with surprise, her mouth opened to protest.

Kent's lips closed over hers with a savage fury. His arms closed around her, drawing her body tightly to his. He seemed to be drawing the very life from her. She pushed against his chest in protest, and her hand found the opening at the neck of his shirt. Her fingertips brushed the rough hair curled on his chest, sending a tingling sensation along her spine. How many times had she watched him, deep in sleep, wondering how it would feel to touch the film of hair that covered his chest, to run her fingertips along his muscular shoulders and arms?

She had intended to resist him. All her senses told her that she must keep him at a distance. But slowly, alarm gave way to a new feeling. Her fingertips moved lazily along his shoulders. Her lips parted to accept his kiss. She swayed weakly against him, molding herself even closer to him.

Still kissing her, Kent leaned against the door. She could feel his body imprinting itself on her own. Then the door was open and Kent carried her through the doorway toward her bed. He dropped her gently against the pillows, then once again crushed her in his arms. Her heart pounded wildly against her chest. Her breathing was ragged and painful.

Abruptly, she was free of him. As she lay, her breath shallow, her heartbeat drumming in her ears, he tore his shirt over his head. Morgan stared at his wide shoulders, the fine hair curling on his chest. As his fingers reached for the buttons on her dress, she was forced back to the reality of the situation.

"What are you doing?" she gasped.

From beneath hooded lids, he regarded her with amusement. "I'm going to share your time off," he said, his fingers fumbling with the buttons.

"No!" She sat up and pushed his hands away.

His lips curled in a smile. "That kiss didn't say no."

"That was a mistake," she said, swinging her legs to the floor and facing him. "One that I don't intend to make again. Leave my room, Kent Taylor. I don't intend to—to play house!" she sputtered. "Now get out of my bedroom!"

In her frustration, tears welled up in her eyes. She stood before him, agitated, disheveled, humiliated.

With his thumb, Kent wiped her cheeks and tilted her chin to face him. Morgan refused to look at him, her wet eyelashes sweeping down over her eyes, spilling fresh tears down her cheeks.

"Morgan," he whispered. "I thought girls like you were extinct." Cupping her face gently in his hands, he bent and kissed away her salty tears.

In that moment of exquisite tenderness, Morgan forced herself to remain motionless, refusing even to meet his gaze, because she knew, suddenly, with blinding clarity, that he would be able to read the love and desire in her eyes. In that brief moment, she would have gladly given herself to him, body and soul.

Feeling the tremors she was fighting to control, he abruptly dropped his hands and strode swiftly to the door, closing it firmly behind him.

She stood where he left her, feeling numbed and cold.

Chapter Six

After their day at the mainland, Morgan became aware of a subtle change in her relationship with Kent.

Kent still spent most of his time polishing the screenplay. Morgan still spent her days as before. But when Kent found fault with her work, he forced himself to mention it more gently. Morgan wasn't certain at first just how to handle this new situation. But each time Kent quietly asked her to retype portions of the manuscript or asked her to explain why she had deviated from his instructions, she found herself smiling. Whatever had happened to him, she liked it. His disposition had definitely improved, and she hoped it would remain that way.

One sunny afternoon Joe delivered a mountain of accumulated mail and newspapers from the States. Kent tossed his mail on his desk and skimmed quickly through several newspapers. Saving them to browse through at a later time, he carefully opened each to the section he wanted. Some he folded open to recent book reviews. Several others were opened to the celebrity gossip columns. He deposited the stack of papers on the night table next to his bed. They would give him something to read before he fell asleep.

Morgan walked to the lodge from her afternoon swim. Still rubbing her damp hair with a towel, she paused in the doorway of her bedroom in surprise. Kent was standing at her dresser with her hand mirror in one hand and a pair of scissors in the other. A mask of foamy shaving cream clung to his chin. He grinned sheepishly.

"I suddenly decided that I look really shabby," he said in explanation. "Then, when I started to shave, I realized how badly I need a haircut. I thought I might borrow your mirror and scissors and trim this mess."

Morgan chuckled. "I don't mind. But don't you think you ought to finish shaving first?"

Kent nodded. "Right. Mind if I use your sink?"

Before Morgan could reply, he walked into her bathroom and began shaving. Without realizing it, she moved closer. There was something so alien about seeing a man dressed in only a pair of jeans, naked to the waist, his feet bare, calmly shaving in her bathroom. She studied the lean hardness of his back and shoulders, the trim, narrow waist. As he rinsed the last of the foam from his face and grabbed a towel, his eyes met hers in the mirror above the sink. She realized with a flush that she had been caught openly staring at him.

"How good a barber are you?" Kent asked her impulsively.

"I—I've never cut a man's hair," she protested.

"Now look," he said, turning to stand in front of her. "I just want a little hair trimmed. And I can't do the back myself. Come on, Morgan," he coaxed. "I'll sit out in the yard, and you can give me a haircut."

After a moment's hesitation, Morgan reluctantly allowed him to catch her hand and lead her to the kitchen. There he grabbed up a chair and carried it outside. Settling himself in a sunny spot, he handed her the scissors.

"Trim away, lady," he said.

Morgan took the towel from her own shoulders and wrapped it about his neck. Tentatively touching his pale hair, she took a deep breath and began combing through the silken strands. After the first few snips with her scissors, she forgot her uneasiness. Soon she was joking and teasing as she trimmed Kent's hair.

As he was admiring her work in the reflected image of the hand mirror, Morgan quipped, "I wonder how you would look with no hair at all. Maybe I'll just slip here and there, and we'll see some pink scalp."

With that, she held up a lock of hair and opened the scissors as if to snip.

With his eyes crinkled in laughter, Kent threatened, "If you dare, I'll paddle your behind."

"You wouldn't dare," she said, again lifting the strand of hair.

"Just try me," he warned.

She had no doubt that he meant what he said. "All right, boss. I'd better quit while I'm ahead. How do you like the job I've done so far?"

Kent held up the mirror and examined his haircut. The bright summer sun glinted on his blond hair, turning it to gleaming gold. Suddenly, all Morgan's senses seemed more alert. She became aware of the clean, spicy scent of his shaving lotion. The smoothness of his freshly shaved face begged to be touched. Morgan ran the comb through the neatly trimmed hair, feeling a sudden shocking current as she realized just how intimate a gesture this was.

Sensing the change in her touch, Kent stood up slowly and faced her. Morgan's hand dropped to her side, still clutching the comb.

Kent reflected, "I ought to keep you around permanently. You have so many hidden talents."

Groping for something—anything—clever to say, she murmured, "I—I've had to learn to do so much on my own. I've had a lot of practice. I always cut my own hair."

Kent's hand stroked the thick mane of her dark hair, lifting a strand and letting it sift gently through his fingers. "It would be a crime to cut this beautiful hair," he said. "It's as black as a raven's wing. And as soft as a baby."

They stood, unmoving, for long seconds, their bodies almost touching. Kent lowered his head and brushed her lips with his. He raised his head and studied her a moment through narrowed eyes. With his hands still at his sides, he again bent his head and kissed her lips gently. Morgan's pulse began to race. The comb dropped from her hand, and of their own volition, her hands circled his waist and moved along the sun-warmed skin of his back.

She felt his sharp intake of breath. Then he enfolded her firmly in the circle of his arms.

"Morgan," he sighed, the name a caress on his lips.

An alarm bell rang in her brain. Each time Kent had held her, his touch had raised her to a new level of desire. For her own safety, she had to keep some distance between them. If she allowed her feelings to get out of hand, she would only regret it later.

She felt his hands moving along her skin sending splinters of pleasure and pain along her spine. She tried to focus her mind on something, anything. A wild confusion of thoughts and sensations collided in her head. She couldn't think, couldn't even protest. Again she seemed distantly aware of little sighs of pleasure, and she knew they were her own; her body was moving dreamlike in his embrace.

Kent's hands, moving over every inch of her body, his lips setting her skin on fire, robbed her of all purpose except to please him. She seemed to have no will, except what he willed. She had found exquisite pleasure in his touch. There was an emptiness in her that only he could fill.

Morgan felt no resistance to his advances. In Kent's arms, she could find paradise on this island.

His searching lips moved down her throat, feeling the fluttering, racing pulse beat, knowing that it was his touch that caused the fever raging through her slender body. His lips moved to the soft roundness of flesh above the top of her bathing suit. His hands found the tie that wound around her neck. The touch of his lips on her skin was a pleasure almost beyond bearing.

With one fluid movement, he swept her up in his powerful arms and carried her to the lodge. He moved swiftly down the hall to his room, where he set her gently on his bed and stretched his long, hard length beside her.

This couldn't be happening to her. She had to resist him. Still, she found herself wantonly sliding her arms about his neck, drawing him toward her. The breeze from the open window couldn't cool the fire that was burning her. Fluttering in the wind, a newspaper wafted from the night table to land on the bed beside her. She turned her head toward the sound.

Leaning above her on one elbow, Kent stroked the side of her face with a finger, coaxing her to turn toward him. She lay still, trying to resist. Slowly, lazily, her head turned, her eyes fastening on his. There was no denying the look on his face. He wanted her. And she knew he could read that same hunger in her eyes. There was no way to soothe the fever that raged out of control through both of them. It was consuming them with its intensity.

His glance was distracted by the rustling of the newspaper beneath her head. He caught at it, intending to toss it aside. But something—some word —caught his eye. He leaned forward tensely, continuing to read, then turned stiffly and sat up on the edge of his bed.

Kneeling behind him, Morgan asked, trembling, "What is it, Kent? What's wrong?"

He shot her an incredulous look. As she attempted to see what he had read, he stood, towering above her, a look of fury darkening his features.

"So! Your friend at the New York *Press* works in the—circulation department!"

Morgan stared at him, bewildered. "Yes."

"I should have known!" he hissed, crumpling the paper into a ball and hurling it savagely against the far wall. "Why do I keep on believing your lies!"

He turned to stare at her still kneeling in the middle of his bed, her hair a tangled cloud of smoky waves about her face. "Look at you! The picture of innocence. What a laugh!" he said, almost to himself. "I should have followed my initial impulse and thrown you out into the night." Like a whip, his words lashed her as he fixed her with a look of cold steel. "You are going to see this job through, Morgan. No matter what. I warned you in the beginning that you would hate me before it was over. Well, you can count on it. Now," and his eyes raked over her contemptuously, "get out of my room. And stay out of my private life!" He caught her roughly by the arm and nearly threw her from the bed.

Confused, stung by his hateful words and blinded by the tears that clouded her vision, Morgan ran down the hall and crawled into her bed, numbed beyond pain.

Chapter Seven

All through the night Morgan lay in her darkened room, seeing Kent's face ablaze with a fury as frightening as anything she had ever witnessed, hearing the hateful words he had hurled at her. She would never know what had sent Kent into that blind rage. But something he had read in the paper, some word, some phrase for which he blamed her personally, had triggered the explosion. She had no idea what it was all about.

Stretched out tautly on her bed, stiff and tense from a night of agonizing images, she curled up under the blanket and tried to erase all the unpleasantness from her mind. Forcing her eyes shut, she lay tensely, reliving in her mind the passionate scene before the anger had dissolved all the joy and beauty from her life.

Morgan felt a tiny shiver of pleasure as she

recalled the touch of Kent's lips on hers, the wild, soaring sensations while locked in his arms. The passion of those few moments was burned in her memory. And with the realization of just how weak her own will was during the moments of passion, Morgan sensed something else—fear. A fear of the power Kent had over her. A fear that even now, despite the awful, unnamed barrier between them, he had the power to bend her to his will if he chose. Morgan realized that she had been drawn into something she was totally unprepared to handle. She had no experience with men like Kent Taylor, men who simply took what they wanted until they tired of it and then moved on to something new to excite them.

How long could she have expected to hold Kent's interest? Morgan covered her face in humiliation. With a sigh, she realized grimly that a man like Kent would probably laugh at her lack of knowledge about men and love and life. A man like Kent, dealing with Hollywood directors, could have his pick of exciting, glamorous women. She would be a fool to think she could have a place in his life or even hold his attention for more than a little while.

Morgan tossed and turned, unable to still her quickened heart. This was such a lonely place. Hidden Island. An appropriate name. And Kent was involved in solitary work. Maybe, just for a moment, the loneliness of his reclusive life had become over-whelming. Morgan flushed at the thought of his touch. His lips, his hands, had aroused her to a fever pitch. If he only knew how tempting his offer of lovemaking had been. Her life was lonely, too.

Morgan had often wondered if she would ever meet a man who would make her feel the way she had felt with Kent. It was so easy to melt into his arms, to allow herself to savor the feeling of being loved and being special to one man.

She stood abruptly to force herself to stop thinking like this. She wasn't special to him. He hated her. And, she reminded herself, she ought to hate him, too. They were absolutely wrong for each other. In fact, the only thing she and Kent Taylor had in common was mutual dislike and distrust. Didn't they argue constantly? And didn't he treat her as though she didn't even exist, except when he wanted something typed, or—and she frowned in anger—when he wanted to taste some good cooking? Yes, she realized suddenly. She was just a convenience. And even that—that tender scene yesterday—had happened merely because she was the only woman available. After all, he had been without the company of a woman for a very long time. She felt certain that when Kent returned to the clamor of his busy life apart from this remote island he probably wouldn't even be able to remember her name.

For the next several days Kent stayed in his room, coming out only when necessary. Morgan found herself listening at her door, straining for any sound of life before attempting to walk down the hall, her fear of running into Kent was so strong. The tension was almost too much to endure. Morgan felt the rift could never be mended now. Whatever Kent thought of her now was stronger even than the passion he had felt before something had distracted him and triggered his explosion of fury. Morgan could only hold on now and hope that the manuscript would soon be completed and she could escape the tension of this island and its complex owner.

It was early evening. Morgan was swimming alone when she spotted the ferry heading very close to their island. Cutting swiftly to shallow water, she stood with her hand shielding the sun from her eyes to watch as the ferry approached the dock of their island.

Now why in the world would the ferry be stopping here? A quick glance at the balcony assured her there was no yellow flag waving in signal. Kent was probably just getting up from his day's sleep. He wouldn't have had a chance to send up the flag yet.

She began to walk toward the dock. Maybe there was a package or message for Kent. Before Morgan could reach the dock, she saw a tall, blond woman stride down the wooden walkway and march along the dock and through the tall weeds toward the lodge. Puzzled, Morgan ran back to gather up her sandals and beach towel. Then she hurried toward the lodge. The ferry pulled up its gate and slowly backed away, leaving a number of large suitcases lined up on the dock. Whoever this woman was, she intended to stay. The ferry was leaving without her.

Walking in the back door, Morgan could hear the cultured voice raised in anger.

". . . Just you and your male secretary for the entire summer, you said! I was to be patient and not disturb our resident genius, you said. And then I hear Reynolds Standish at a party telling friends about you and your velvet-voiced little 'secretary' all alone here for the summer. Well, darling, I was not born yesterday, you know. I'm not about to move over and let some dull-witted little typist move into my territory."

Kent's voice was low and surprisingly quiet. "I am not anybody's territory, Audrey. You say Standish told the entire gathering that I was alone here with a young woman?" He seemed thoughtful, then added, "I made it quite plain that I didn't want you here while I worked. You're getting back on that ferry tomorrow."

"Now, darling . . ." She stopped as she saw Kent's eyes move past her to the doorway.

Turning, the elegant blond woman studied Morgan, who was poised on the threshold as if ready to run from her scrutiny.

Unconsciously, Morgan drew the beach towel tighter about her skimpy, wet bathing suit. Beads of water dripped from her hair to her eyelashes and down her cheeks. She studied the woman who stood openly scowling at her. Standing there beside Kent, Morgan realized with a shock that they were like a pair of matched bookends. Each of them was tall, tanned, blond, perfectly proportioned. Despite the windy ride on the ferry, the woman's hair was perfectly coiffed. Not a hair was out of place. She had a fabulous tan. A California tan. She was wearing a slim skirt that showed off her long, trim, elegant legs. There were no scratches from brambles on those legs, thought Morgan wryly.

"Well, Kent, are you going to introduce me to your secretary?" the woman demanded.

"Audrey Allen, this is Morgan Anders."

Morgan accepted the handshake and noted that the nails were long and perfectly manicured. She caught the woman staring at her own stubby nails. Clutching the towel with one hand, Morgan drew her other hand behind her back.

"It's nice to meet you, Miss Allen. Excuse me. I'll get dressed."

Morgan backed out of the room and nearly ran down the hall in her eagerness to get away from this immaculate woman. But before she could reach her bedroom door, she couldn't help hearing Audrey say, "Well, that's a relief, darling. Even in such a dreary place as this, I don't think a man like you could find something as drab as that very tempting."

Morgan slammed the bedroom door and kicked her bed. Drab! How dare that glittering phony call her drab! Seething, she stepped under the shower and furiously scrubbed her hair. Half an hour later, with steam rolling about her room, Morgan plugged in her hair dryer and dug out the hair rollers she hadn't bothered to use since she had arrived on the island. Then, with her hair in curlers, she carefully applied makeup, something else she had barely thought about since her arrival. When her makeup was finished, she slipped into the lovely silk dress she had worn on her drive through Canada. She brushed her long, dark hair into soft curls and surveyed her reflection in the mirror. She sighed. It was the best she could do. And that perfect creature in the other room was probably wearing something expensive and very sexy for dinner tonight. With one last glance in the mirror, Morgan opened the door and walked boldly down the hall.

The house was silent.

She peered into the dimly lit dining room, then made her way to the kitchen. The light hanging above the table had been turned on, illuminating a roughly scrawled note. Morgan recognized Kent's handwriting.

It read: "Tapped on your door. No reply. Gone to mainland. Back late."

Morgan straightened up and stared around the room. What a ridiculous, humiliating situation! Here she was, looking as glamorous as she could possibly look, and there was no one to admire her. In disgust, she crumpled up the note and hurled it against the refrigerator. Turning on her heel, she stomped down the hall toward her room. Staring at her reflection in the mirror, she suddenly flung herself across the bed and allowed the bitter tears of anger and frustration to flow freely. Once started, the tears became a torrent. Her body racked with sobs. What a horrible woman Audrey Allen was! She had said mean, hurtful words. And she had come racing to the island to get her clutches on Kent Taylor. Now they were at some dimly lit restaurant. Maybe they were even driving to the little French castle where Kent had taken her on their romantic day off.

Suddenly, startled by a new thought, she sat up. How had they managed to go to the mainland? It was dark outside, and the ferry had passed hours ago. There was no way to contact Joe for the launch. So how had Kent and Audrey gotten off this island?

Then she began to cry again. It didn't matter. All that mattered was that that awful woman had come here.

Biting her lip, Morgan undressed and washed off her makeup. Dressed in only a delicately embroidered nightgown, she padded barefoot to the kitchen and made herself a cup of tea. Plumping up her pillows, she sat cross-legged in the bed and sipped the hot brew. Let them go to the mainland. Let Kent take Audrey to some romantic little place. It certainly didn't matter to her what those two did. Kent Taylor meant nothing to her, anyway. What he did was his own business.

An hour later Morgan was still sitting in her bed, shuffling a deck of cards for another lonely game of solitaire. Nibbling a peanut butter sandwich, she told herself for the hundredth time that she wasn't the least bit tired. And she didn't care how late Kent Taylor came home. It didn't bother her at all. As her lids grew heavier, she leaned back against the pillows. She would just close her eyes for a moment. It wasn't that she wanted to spy on Kent and Audrey. But she was curious to see how they got off the island. If it weren't for that curiosity, she told herself, she would just go to sleep. But not yet. Not quite yet.

Morgan was instantly awake. The room was unusually dark. She was aware of a strange sound. Rain pattered against the curtained window and drummed on the roof of the lodge. Morgan knew it was irrational to blame the weather on Audrey Allen, but it gave her a perverse pleasure to think that even the skies were protesting her jarring presence on this peaceful paradise. "The angels are weeping," her grandfather used to claim whenever it rained. After endless days of sunshine, Audrey had brought ominous, dark storm clouds to mar the bliss of Hidden Island.

Bliss! What a joke. There were only anger and tension and hostility here. The joy she had found in Kent's arms had been forever shattered.

Morgan suddenly sat up, remembering something shocking. Had it been only a dream last night or. . . ? No, she could vaguely recall the touch of a hand lifting her head and cradling it gently against the pillows. The deck of cards had been deftly swept aside, and a blanket was spread over her. And she could recall something else, or perhaps she had dreamed it. Her name had been murmured softly as a kiss had brushed her temple.

Oh no! She had fallen asleep with the cards still spread on the bed and the light still burning on her night table. And Kent had found her and covered her for the night. Her cheeks flamed at the thought of how she must have looked: eyes smudged from crying like a baby, her hair in disarray and maybe her nightgown as well. She suddenly felt so foolish. How must she have looked to Kent? Sound asleep sitting back against the headboard. A deck of cards spread about. And nothing but a flimsy nightgown to cover her nakedness. Had he and Audrey shared a laugh about her childish behavior? It galled Morgan to think that maybe Audrey had stood in the doorway, watching, sharing a laugh with Kent—at her expense.

In exasperation, Morgan buried her face in her hands and groaned. Maybe, if she were lucky, Kent and Audrey would both sleep late and she could spend the afternoon out of sight. But where? If the rain continued all day, she couldn't even leave the lodge. Well, she thought glumly, she could always stay in her bedroom all day. But for now, she would fix herself some breakfast. After a late night, Kent and Audrey wouldn't be up at this early hour. Tying the sash of her soft pink robe, Morgan made her way quietly to the kitchen.

As butter melted in a skillet, Morgan spread jam on a piece of toast. The weather outside was as gray as her mood. She absently tucked a stray strand of hair behind her ear and broke an egg into a dish. At the sound of footsteps, she whirled.

"You! What are you doing up so early?" she asked in surprise, feeling the flush of embarrassment begin to burn her cheeks.

Wearing jeans and a pale blue sweater over a checked shirt, he peered into the skillet, ignoring her question. "An egg. Just what I wanted." He looked up, his face a bland mask. "I've been up for hours. How about you?" His voice flowed smoothly, like warm honey. It infuriated her.

"No. I—I just woke up a few minutes ago."

His cold, amber eyes were boring into her. She turned her back on him and broke another egg. He probably wanted her to ask about his evening with Audrey. Morgan was dying to know how they managed to get to the mainland and back. But she wasn't going to give him the satisfaction of asking. Her movements were stiff and tense.

As if reading her mind, Kent remarked as he glanced out the window, "We were lucky to get back here before the rain started. How was your evening, Morgan?"

"Oh, terrific," she said sarcastically. "After a lavish peanut butter sandwich, I enjoyed several rousing games of solitaire. I can't think when I've had more fun."

With that, she angrily stabbed at the eggs, flipping one onto each plate. Without glancing at him, she set the plate before him and sat down.

Kent's face was unreadable, but she could hear the suppressed laughter as he muttered, "I could see that you had too much excitement. It finally wore you out and put you to sleep."

Refusing to meet his eyes, she said in a near whisper, "I realized this morning that someone must have covered me after I fell asleep."

"*Ummm.* You sleep in a most charming night-gown," he said.

Morgan scraped back her chair and got up to attend to the toast and escape his eyes. He was laughing at her, and she couldn't think of a quick response.

As she bent to eat, Kent said quietly, "I'm sorry about last night, Morgan. I knocked on your bedroom door to see if you wanted to join us. I couldn't figure out whether you were really in the shower all that time or if you were just ignoring me. But Audrey was in such a bad mood, I really didn't think you would enjoy her company."

"You were right," she said without further comment. She wouldn't bother to admit that she was spending all that time in her room trying to make herself as glamorous as possible in order to compete with that awful woman. Had Kent noticed the softly curled hair and traces of makeup when he stood over her bed last night?

"Audrey was so determined to go somewhere that she had even arranged for a boat before she boarded the ferry. I almost refused to go along with her plans, but then I decided that you would be better off without her nasty tongue for the evening."

"Well, how kind of you, Kent, to worry about drab little me," Morgan snapped. "But as I told you, I had a perfectly wonderful time without either of you. And maybe Audrey Allen can—can please you without sending you into a rage." With that, Morgan dumped her dishes in the sink and strode across the room.

Before she could reach the door, Kent's hand closed around her arm, turning her to face him. Instinctively, her other hand came up to strike him. Kent easily caught it and pinned it firmly behind her. She turned her face away to hide the tears that were threatening to spill from her eyes. Holding both her hands behind her back in one of his hands, he caught her chin and forced her to look at him. His face was as ominous as a storm cloud.

"That comment was beneath you, Morgan," he said quietly.

"Really! How could you be the judge of that, since nothing is beneath you?" she hissed.

His eyes narrowed. Morgan refused to flinch under his scrutiny. She met his gaze squarely. His angry breath fanned across her cheek. She could see the struggle Kent was waging within himself. Suddenly, without warning, his head lowered and his mouth claimed hers in a fierce kiss, grinding her lips against her teeth. With her hands still held behind her back, Morgan was defenseless.

She forced herself to remain rigid. When he lifted his head, she scorched him with a look of contempt. She wanted to punish him for all the hateful things he had said, all the times he had hurt her. She would not give him the satisfaction of showing him how she really felt.

Scornfully, she rasped, "Does it make you happy to force yourself on me?"

Once again, his eyes narrowed, and she saw the tiny flames appear around the pupils. With deliberate calm, Kent slowly, lazily bent his head to her. This time, the kiss he offered was gentle, teasing, coaxing her to respond. She continued holding herself rigid, desperately wanting to hide from him her true feelings. It was useless. Her control began to slip as Kent released her hands and began a slow, leisurely exploration of her body. Morgan leaned weakly against the door, holding her fists tightly at her sides. His probing lips found the pulse beat at the base of her throat. He held his lips to the spot, feeling the wildly racing pulse, and knew instantly that for all her control his kiss was having the desired effect on her.

Kent dropped his hands and studied her face. Morgan met his gaze, then turned and fled down the hall to her room.

* * *

After showering and dressing, Morgan moved aimlessly about her room. It was apparent that Audrey had no intention of getting out of bed in time to catch the morning ferry.

In her office an hour later, as Morgan bent over her typing table, peering in disgust at a completely illegible line of Kent's writing, Audrey strode confidently across the room.

"So. This is where you work," she said breezily. "At least Kent had the good sense to stick you away from the main section of the lodge," she said smugly.

Morgan's head shot up. She stared, momentarily speechless, at the figure in front of her. Audrey's hair was perfectly arranged, looking as though she had just stepped out of the hairdresser's. She carefully had applied her makeup, with her eyes heavily outlined with liner and mascara. Ruby lips glistened with a thick coating of gloss. Dressed in black lounging pants and a glittering chiffon top, she looked as though she were appearing on a movie set instead of spending the day at a wilderness lodge.

Morgan suppressed a smile and said calmly, "Kent didn't pick this room for my work. I did."

With that, she once more bent her head and pondered the paper on her typing table, effectively shutting out the intruder. Audrey seemed not to notice her deliberate snub. She moved slowly around the room, picking up a book on the coffee table and examining the page marked. Then she walked behind Morgan and began to read over her shoulder.

Gritting her teeth, Morgan said icily, "I'm sure you'll excuse me, Miss Allen. I have quite a bit of work to do." With that, she picked up the pile of papers and swiveled her typing chair away from Audrey's scrutiny.

Shrugging, Audrey said, "Kent said you are to accompany us on a cruise along the coast."

Her words weren't spoken invitingly. In fact, Morgan was sure that Audrey felt like choking on that invitation. She was about to politely refuse when Kent appeared in the doorway.

"Get your things, Morgan. The charter boat will be here soon." His eyes dared her to argue with him. Without a word, Morgan brushed past him to go to her room.

When the charter boat sounded its horn at the dock, Morgan had slipped into a comfortable pair of deck shoes and simple cotton slacks and a summery shirt. With a quick brush through her hair, she was ready for a day of sightseeing. She had been eager to see more of the countryside, but, she thought wryly, not in the company of Audrey Allen. Morgan forced a thin smile on her lips and joined Audrey and Kent on the dock.

Audrey had tied an expensive scarf about her hair, and her eyes were completely hidden by enormous sunglasses. She stood aside as Morgan jumped aboard the boat, then made her entrance clutching Kent's arm and accepting a helping hand from the captain of the boat, who seemed much impressed by her exotic appearance.

The boat made a leisurely path along the Northumberland Strait, following the rugged shoreline.

Morgan stood at the railing, feeling the exhilaration of the gentle wind ruffling her hair.

Audrey seemed completely disinterested in the beauty of the countryside. She was holding both Kent and the captain enthralled with her endless stories of travel to the far ends of the earth.

Morgan was staring at a tiny cove, its white sand sparkling in the sunlight, wondering if it could be the spot where she and Kent had walked barefoot along the shore.

His deep voice, so near her ear, startled her. "Have you spotted it yet?"

"What?" She turned and found his eyes boring into her. She looked away, refusing to meet his gaze. "Have I spotted what yet?" she asked, feigning innocence.

"Our private beach," he murmured.

"They all look the same," she said flatly. She didn't want to talk to him about private beaches. Not when Audrey was being so entertaining.

"No, they don't," he said, moving closer and pointing to the distant shore. "Our beach curled in a sort of half-moon," he explained. "And to one side stood a giant boulder, half-submerged in the surf. Don't you remember?"

"Of course I remember," she snapped.

Ignoring her outburst, he touched her shoulder. "Look. Over there. That one is our beach."

She looked where he pointed, unable to think about anything but the warmth where his hand was touching her.

"What do you two find so fascinating?" Audrey asked, suddenly appearing at Kent's side. She wrapped her hands possessively around his arm, smiling up into his face.

"An interesting looking cove," Kent replied.

Audrey studied Morgan's grim face. "I don't think our little secretary is enjoying this, Kent," she said smugly. "Are we feeling seasick, Morgan?" she asked solicitously.

"We feel just fine," Morgan said sarcastically. "Excuse me." She made her way to the other side of the boat, leaving Kent and Audrey alone.

When the captain called their attention to an interesting little fishing village, Morgan found herself pressed between Kent and Audrey at the railing. Feeling his shoulder brushing hers, she felt her heart begin its hammering.

Morgan forced herself to ignore Kent and Audrey and concentrate on the passing scenery. This land was so rugged and beautiful. An artist could never do it justice. The waters along the coast were a brilliant azure, darkening to cobalt farther out toward the middle of the strait. The brilliant sun reflected off the crest of waves, frosting them with golden splashes of color.

The charter boat docked for lunch at Cardigan Bay. Kent insisted that the captain join them for their meal. In spite of her unhappiness, Morgan had to smile at the eagerness with which the captain accepted the invitation. He couldn't hide his fascination with Audrey Allen. Audrey was enjoying the captain's attentions, although she still kept her eye on Kent as well.

The mouth-watering scent of fresh seafood lured their party to a wonderful old restaurant overlooking the picturesque bay. They sat near a window watching the colorful sailboats that dotted the calm waters. A group of youngsters on horseback frolicked in the gentle surf along the shore. Old men, their skin turned to leather by the ravages of sun and wind, sat mending their nets, enjoying the brilliant sun, exchanging fish stories.

Morgan was uncomfortably aware of the length of Kent's thigh brushing hers in the booth. She darted a glance at Audrey, who was busy telling the captain a funny story.

Softly, so the others wouldn't hear, Morgan muttered to Kent, "Must you sit so close?"

"Would you like me to sit on the floor?" he said, an angry gleam in his eyes.

She turned away, trying to ignore him, but it was impossible. The captain spoke to Kent, and he leaned across Morgan to reply. She jumped at the contact with him. He shot her a murderous look, then leaned even closer. Morgan sighed. It was so hot in here. And she was so edgy. She just wanted to be alone. To be free of Kent's touch and his eyes, boring into her, and his voice, lulling her into a false sense of security with its honey richness.

As they made their way back to the charter boat, Kent caught Morgan's elbow when she stumbled, and once again she felt her senses reeling from his touch. Abruptly, she pulled her arm free and strode on ahead.

During the long afternoon, Morgan stayed by the railing, watching the passing scenery, hearing Audrey's constant stream of chatter, hearing her occasional bursts of laughter. When Hidden Island finally came into view, Morgan felt herself relax. Home. The thought shocked her. This wasn't her home. Now why did she suddenly think such a thing? She didn't belong here. And when she left, she would never see this island again. Still, seeing it draw nearer, she felt her heartbeat quicken. It would be so good to be able to go to her room and shut out the sounds of Audrey's voice, to escape Kent's tawny eyes, which were always studying her.

When they docked, Morgan had to force herself not to bolt and run. She thanked the captain, smiled as he gave her a hand up to the dock and walked slowly toward the lodge. All the while, she was aware that Kent was watching her. She held her head high, refusing to meet his eyes.

Before she left, Audrey had persuaded the captain to pick them up for a trip to the mainland at dinnertime. Morgan begged off, insisting she had a headache. One glance at Kent's stormy features told her he didn't believe her.

In her room Morgan showered and drew on a thin summer wrap. It felt wonderful to wash away the grime of the day and to relax alone on her bed. A short time later there was a brief knock on her bedroom door. Then the door was thrown open, and Kent filled the doorway.

"Get dressed, Morgan. You're going with us to dinner," he ordered curtly.

"I am not," she said, swinging her legs to the floor and standing to face him.

He strode across the room to the closet and fumbled through the clothing hanging there. Spying the rose-colored silk dress, he tossed it across the foot of the bed. "Here. Put this on. And be ready in an hour."

"I will not." She faced him, small and defiant, her hands on her hips, her chin jutting out.

Kent towered above her. Seeing her so small yet so determined, he wanted to laugh. If she were anyone else, it would have been amusing. But this child-woman had the ability to get under his skin in a way no one else ever could. He caught her by the wrist and ran his fingers along the low neckline of the sheer wrap. "If I have to, I'll tear this thing off you and dress you myself," he muttered.

Her eyes grew round in shock. "You wouldn't dare!"

As he reached for the sash at her waist, she backed away from him. "Stop it, Kent!" As he moved nearer, she held up her hands in a gesture of defeat. "All right. I'll get dressed. Now get out of my room."

His lips curled in the faintest hint of a smile, and he turned and stalked away.

Morgan slammed drawers, flung her wrap across the bed, and took out her fury on everything in the room. An hour later she emerged, hair softly curled, makeup applied, and the lovely rose silk dress gently molding her slim curves. She moved self-consciously down the hallway, teetering in the long-unused, high-heeled sandals.

Kent and Audrey were entertaining the captain in the dining room. Morgan noticed that a bar had been set up, and there was the clink of ice in glasses. She paused uncertainly in the doorway, feeling suddenly awkward. Three heads swiveled to study her.

"My, don't we look pretty," Audrey said.

"We thank you," Morgan shot back, instantly regretting her sarcasm. Why did she have to be so defensive with this woman?

Kent was standing on the far side of the room, his face in shadow.

As Morgan moved closer to the group, Audrey said, "I was just telling the captain an interesting story."

"Don't let me interrupt you," Morgan said. "Please go on."

As the conversation resumed, Kent walked up to Morgan with a glass of wine. "You look lovely," he murmured.

"Thank you," she said stiffly.

"And thank you for coming," he said gently. "I'm sorry about that scene."

"Which scene are you referring to, Kent? There have been so many."

His features grew hard. "I take it back. I'm not sorry about that scene—or any of them," he said, handing her the glass.

She accepted the wine with trembling hands. How was she possibly going to get through the evening? As the others talked, Morgan studied them through lowered lashes.

Audrey was elegant, as always. She was wearing softly flowing lounging pajamas and a matching top cut very low at the neckline to reveal the top of her full, ripe bosom. Draped casually across a chair was a matching fringed shawl of expensive cut velvet. Her blond hair had been swept up in a sophisticated knot. The earrings gleaming at her earlobes had to be real diamonds. The entire effect was stunning.

The captain had changed from his working clothes to a very well-cut suit. With his rugged good looks and his darkly tanned and weathered skin against sun-kissed sandy hair, he cut a handsome figure.

Morgan could barely look at Kent. He took her breath away. He had on a light-colored linen sport coat over dark slacks and a dark shirt open at the throat. The collar of his dark shirt contrasted with his pale, silky hair. He appeared casual and in control, calmly surveying his guests.

When they made their way to the boat, Morgan moved stiffly along with the others, feeling completely isolated from their group.

The captain boasted of knowing a marvelous little spot for dinner. Trusting his judgment, the others deferred to him. On the ride across the strait, Morgan sat back, allowing the conversation to flow around her. At Port Elgin the charter boat followed the coastline and stopped at a wharf. Along the wharf was a huge, old warehouse, which had been modernized and converted into lovely import shops. At the very top of the building was a glass-enclosed restaurant with a view of the water for miles. Warm, wood paneling, a gleaming copper-hooded fireplace and the lights from dozens of boats in the water gave the room a cozy atmosphere. In the corner of the room a piano player offered popular requests. The conversation was muted. The effect was elegant yet comfortable.

A waiter led them to a quiet booth overlooking the black expanse of the Northumberland Strait.

The wall of glass gave the dining room the effect of being right on the water. Morgan found herself seated beside Kent, facing the captain; beside him, facing Kent, was Audrey. She had hoped to put the table between herself and Kent. Now she would have to endure an entire evening fighting off the strong feelings his presence always brought on.

The captain was enjoying his role as guide. He poured the wine, suggested a special salad, and even recommended specialties of the house. Morgan forced herself to relax, allowing the conversation to flow around her while she leaned back and watched the play of lights from the boats on the darkened water. The piano player was playing a sad, haunting melody, and Morgan paused in her thoughts to recall the words of the song. It was about one man who could mend a broken heart. Morgan realized she had heard hundreds of songs with that theme, and for the first time the words had meaning for her.

While the talk hummed about her, Morgan felt Kent's eyes on her. She turned her head and found him watching her, a questioning look on his face.

"Well? Do you?" he asked.

She stared at him, uncomprehending. "Do I what?" she asked.

"Do you care to dance?" he said. "This is the second time I've asked you. Where have you been?"

"I—a million miles away," she lied. She had been here, beside him, fighting an almost overwhelming desire to clutch his arm.

He stood. "Come on, Morgan."

"No." She was back in control.

"Oh, for heaven's sake, Kent. I'll dance with you," Audrey said in exasperation.

They moved to the small dance floor. Morgan and the captain watched them in silence for a few minutes.

"She's beautiful!" breathed the captain.

"Yes. She is," Morgan admitted tonelessly.

"She's been telling me all about herself. But then I'm sure you already know she's an actress," he said, impressed.

"No." Morgan stifled an urge to add that she was certain Audrey enjoyed talking about herself, especially with such an appreciative audience.

Morgan watched Kent and Audrey. They were a stunning couple. All eyes in the room were on them. When they returned to the table, Kent smiled down easily into Audrey's beaming, upturned face.

"After dinner it's your turn, captain," Audrey said as though bestowing a special favor. She was thoroughly enjoying having two attentive males.

"With pleasure," the captain replied.

Morgan ate the wonderful meal without tasting it. The wine, the marvelous salad of fresh garden greens and the freshly caught seafood were moved listlessly about her plate in the hopes that no one would notice her lack of appetite.

Audrey kept up a running patter, and Morgan realized that if she smiled when the others smiled and nodded occasionally, no one would notice that she wasn't really listening. Soon it became a game to see if she could carry off the pretense for the entire evening. Morgan began to relax. It even helped to take her mind off Kent. But not for long. When the meal ended, Audrey and the captain walked to the dance floor. Kent stood, and Morgan realized she had no choice but to accept his offer to dance. He took her hand in his and led her to the floor.

She felt a shock as his arm circled her waist. Very lightly, she dropped her hand at his shoulder, barely touching him. She moved stiffly, unwilling to let him see how his touch was affecting her. Neither of them spoke. They simply moved among the other couples. Morgan stared at a spot somewhere behind him, so aware of his lips near her temple, she couldn't think.

"How did you like dinner?" he asked, his breath warm across her cheek.

She had to tip her head back to reply. Her eyes met his, and she found that she couldn't look away. "It was fine," she lied. She couldn't remember a single thing she had eaten.

"Liar," he said softly against her hair.

She stiffened. "What? Kent . . ."

"Don't talk, Morgan," he said, his lips warm against her temple. "Just let me hold you."

His hand moved about her waist to mold her tighter to him. Her hand slid along his shoulder as she snuggled against his chest. Kent rubbed his chin over the top of her head, then brought his lips once more to rest against her throbbing temple. Morgan thought her bones would melt. If Kent continued holding her this gently, her knees would soon turn to rubber and he would have to carry her off the dance floor. But for all her trembling, she managed to sway softly with him in time to the music.

When the song ended, they made their way silently back to their table to join Audrey and the captain.

Later, Kent and Audrey danced, and Morgan danced with the captain. And when the evening ended, they returned to the boat for the ride back to Hidden Island.

The moon was a golden orb in the blackened sky. A million diamond stars glittered, reflecting in the darkened waves, weaving ribbons of light that trailed across the water.

When the boat docked at their island, Morgan thanked the captain for his pleasant company and made her way beside Kent and Audrey along the path toward the lodge. In her room, as she undressed, she paused at the window to watch the dark outline of the charter boat make its way back across the wide stretch of water.

Drifting off to sleep, she heard the familiar sound of Kent's furious pacing in the other room. Briefly she pondered his puzzling, lightning-swift changes of mood.

Chapter Eight

Morgan stared at the pile of pages on her typing table. Kent had managed to turn out an enormous amount of work in one night. The man was unbelievable.

After several cups of coffee she forced herself to begin typing. This was going to be a busy day.

It was late morning before Audrey Allen made her presence felt. She swept into Morgan's office wearing exotic silk pants and a matching halter top. While Morgan typed, she explored every inch of the office, pausing before Morgan's shell collection, fingering the handwritten pages of Kent's manuscript, then replacing them to pick up the typewritten pages Morgan had just completed.

Looking up in disgust at the interruption, Morgan asked irritably, "Is there something I can do for you, Audrey?"

"Not a thing," Audrey said sweetly. "I just thought I'd browse in here while I wait for Kent."

"Wait for Kent?" Morgan looked skeptical. "He'll probably sleep all day. As you can see by this mound of papers, he worked throughout the night."

"I just passed his room on my way here," Audrey said cheerfully. "I reminded him the boat should be here shortly."

"The boat?" Morgan stared at the woman in surprise.

"You don't think I'm going to sit around this dreary little place all day, do you?" Audrey said. "I've asked the captain to come around." After the briefest hesitation, she added, "Are you coming with us, Morgan?"

Morgan glanced at the pile of papers before her. She was torn between wanting to see the countryside with Kent and dreading a repeat of yesterday's highly charged emotions. Pretending to be too busy seemed the easiest solution.

"I think I'd better stay here. This typing might take hours," Morgan said.

"Oh, what a shame," Audrey said and sighed dramatically.

Morgan glanced up in time to see the victorious smile on Audrey's face before she turned away. Gritting her teeth in frustration, she returned to her typing.

Later, as Kent and Audrey appeared in the doorway, Morgan glanced up. Kent's familiar, rumpled attire had once again been exchanged for a perfectly tailored pair of beige slacks and a dark sweater over a beige silk shirt. His tawny eyes met Morgan's for a moment before he turned to Audrey.

"We're off now," Audrey called cheerfully. Smiling, she looked up into Kent's face. "We probably won't be back until after dinner, will we, darling?"

"I'm not sure, Audrey," he said. "Just what have you and the captain planned this time?"

"Why, darling, I want to see more of your precious Canadian landscape. I want to see everything. Such romantic names: Cardigan Bay, Murray Harbor. Maybe we can tour a bustling, modern little city—Moncton, or even Fredericton."

Clutching Kent's arm, she steered him down the hallway. Her voice trailed back to Morgan. "You get so dull, stuck here on this desolate little island, darling. I'm sure your secretary can manage just fine without having us interrupting her work."

Morgan heard the door slam, and the trill of Audrey's laughter filtered on the breeze as the two made their way toward the dock. Morgan walked to the window in time to see them board the charter boat. It was obvious that Audrey thought of every detail. And she would have two admirers all to herself.

Morgan was puzzled. When she had first walked into the lodge after Audrey's arrival, she had heard Kent telling her that she would have to leave. Now, Audrey was not only still here, but Kent was abandoning his work just to show her around New Brunswick. Morgan wondered what had happened to make Kent change his mind. Seeing Audrey again, had he suddenly realized just how much he had missed her this summer?

Standing at the huge bay window, she watched the waves roll along the white, sandy beach. Her mind was in a turmoil. Audrey Allen was a stunning woman. There was no doubt about that. What man in his right mind wouldn't notice her? And Morgan certainly couldn't pretend to know what went on in Kent Taylor's mind. But he had seemed so dedicated to completing his screenplay as quickly as possible. And now, here he was, escorting Audrey around New Brunswick like a summer tourist.

She turned from the window and hurried back to her small office. She wasted too much time thinking about those two. They were none of her business. But nagging questions persisted. Did Audrey Allen have some influence in the movie business? After all, Kent was a struggling screenwriter. Maybe he needed Audrey's goodwill to succeed. Morgan chewed her pencil and allowed her thoughts to wander. Would Kent cultivate Audrey's friendship—and more—just to get ahead? Why else would he allow her to stay on when he had earlier ordered her to leave? Morgan sighed. All these questions were so upsetting. And the answer was probably just as she had thought earlier—that Kent suddenly realized just how much he had missed Audrey. They were a dazzling couple.

After an hour of hard work Morgan pushed her typing chair aside and hurried from the room. She didn't like the troubling thoughts that kept creeping into her mind. She would finish typing later. Right now she was going for a cold swim in the lake.

Later, toweling herself dry on the white beach, Morgan's eyes trailed to the raft anchored in deep water. She shivered as she recalled the shock of feeling Kent's touch for the first time. Her thoughts drifted to that night in her room and the afternoon she had trimmed his hair. With Audrey Allen now on the scene, she was relieved that nothing serious had occurred between them. It would have been an intolerable situation if she had given in to the passion of those moments and then had to watch Audrey casually stroll back into his life. Now at least she could hold her head up and pretend that it didn't matter. She would simply continue to try to act as though Kent Taylor meant nothing at all to her.

Morgan made her way to the lodge, dismissing any thought of food. She had lost her appetite. The sun was making its arc across the western skyline. She sighed. The day seemed much longer without Kent's temper and the familiar pattern of his work. She hadn't realized just how much of her day revolved around Kent Taylor and his needs.

Slamming the back door much harder than was necessary, Morgan told herself that she should be grateful for this free time. Consider it a well-earned vacation, she consoled herself. But the thoughts persisted. In just these short summer weeks her life had altered. She had become accustomed to the whims of this short-tempered, obstinate, ambitious man. And her life would never again be the same.

That evening, to ward off the chill, Morgan made a fire in the huge, stone fireplace. Curling up with her book, she forced herself to concentrate on the words. She would not allow herself to think about Kent and Audrey. With great effort, she managed to read several chapters. Then, in frustration, she carefully banked the fire and went to her bedroom. This time she made certain that the light was out, the door was closed and that she was modestly covered with a blanket. She wasn't about to look like a helpless little child again. After fitfully tossing and turning for awhile, she fell into a sound sleep at last, completely shutting out the sounds of Kent and Audrey's late return.

In the stillness before dawn, Morgan was abruptly awakened. She lay a moment, listening for the sound of Kent's movements. The sound of him moving about the room, pacing, typing, had become part of Morgan's normal routine. Often she awoke during the night, listened for a moment to the familiar sound, and drifted back into sleep, comforted by the thought that Kent was working in the other room. But this morning there was just silence. Disturbed by the break in routine, she sat up. Convinced that Kent had probably completed his work for the night and had gone to sleep, or else was still on the mainland with Audrey, Morgan padded silently down the hallway toward the kitchen. Without a robe to cover her filmy nightgown, she shivered in the damp chill. She was eager to get a drink of water and hurry back to the warmth of her bed.

As she passed through the dining room, a movement by the window startled her. Gasping, she shrank back against the wall, then expelled her breath slowly, as she identified the tall outline of Kent.

"What are you doing up?" he asked sharply.

"Kent! You scared the life out of me," she sighed.

"I couldn't sleep. I thought I'd get a drink of water." She stared at his towering figure dimly illuminated against the windowpane. "I didn't hear you pacing out here," she whispered. "I thought either you were still out with Audrey or you'd gone to bed."

Running a hand through his tousled hair, he said, "I was having trouble with a scene. I've just been standing here by the bay window, trying to work it out in my mind."

His eyes trailed slowly over her, taking in her bare feet, the filmy, opaque nightgown barely concealing the soft curves of her slim figure, then stopping to rest on the dark cloud of hair spilling about her face and shoulders.

Morgan was grateful that the darkness hid her flush of embarrassment. Turning swiftly, she hurried through the doorway and took refuge in the kitchen. For several minutes she ran the tap at the sink, hoping to give herself time to calm her racing heartbeat.

Emerging from the kitchen, she crossed the hall and stopped short. Kent had stirred the ashes in the fireplace and had added more kindling. A fire blazed in the darkened room, throwing eerie shadows across the walls and ceiling. As she drew near the fire, he walked from the shadows carrying a log. The flames hissed as he tossed the log on the grate. For a moment, the flames flickered, dimmed, then rose as they licked along the bark and engulfed the log. Kent wiped his palms on his jeans, then straightened to tower over Morgan.

Pinpoints of flame were reflected in his eyes. They

stood, nearly touching, feeling the warmth of the fire kiss their skin.

Nervously, Morgan licked her lips. His eyes lingered on her mouth.

"Have you worked out your problem with the scene?" she asked.

"No." He stared down at her. "Think you'll be able to get back to sleep?"

She shook her head. "Not now. I'm too wide awake."

The movement of her head fluttered her hair softly. Kent's hand reached out, gently lifting a strand from her cheek. The touch was a caress. The hint of a smile left her lips, replaced by a puzzled, expectant look. Their eyes met, seeking, questioning. The air between them seemed alive with an electric current.

Without a word, Kent enfolded her in his arms. Morgan seemed to have no will of her own. She swayed toward him, her heart seeming to burst as his lips brushed the top of her head, then moved along her temple. She tipped her head far back to meet his lips.

Time stopped. Morgan was aware only of the strength of his hands as they moved along her body, molding her closer still to him. She could feel the warmth of him burning through the thin fabric of her nightgown.

Slowly, as his kiss deepened, she was aware of new sensations. A tingle of pleasure curled along her spine. Sighing, Morgan slid her hand down his chest, where her fingertips felt the savage pounding of his heart. Suddenly aware of the power she had over him, feeling the hard, driving need of his emotions, Morgan seemed to surrender to her own awakening, and she melted against him.

Holding her a little away from him, Kent gave her a smoldering look. With a muttered "Morgan," he pulled her roughly against him. Her breasts were crushed against the granite wall of his chest. Her lips opened to receive his kiss as her hands sought the strength of his shoulders. With his hands entwined in the thick tangle of her hair, their bodies fused together in raw hunger.

His lips moved over her face, raining kisses on her cheeks and temple, nibbling an earlobe, then sliding down to the base of her throat, feeling her pulse hammering painfully.

A searing, driving need heightened all her senses, making her aware of the male scent of him, the slightly salty taste as she brought her lips to rest in the hollow of his throat, where his pounding pulse beat revealed his own racing emotions. Her fingertips moved gently along the fine film of golden hair covering his chest, sending shock waves colliding in her mind.

When at last Kent lifted his head, he groaned and buried his face in her hair. Softly, he whispered, "The next time you wake up in the night, you'd better stay in your room. With the door locked."

With his thumb and forefinger he lifted her chin and stared at her lips, still moist and parted from his kiss. He brushed his thumb across her cheek, and Morgan turned her face to follow the movement.

"Kent, I . . ."

With his fingers pressed against her lips, he silenced her.

She felt a longing she had never before known. A need shuddering through her slender body that he could feel as he tightened his grip on her tense shoulders.

Bending, he brushed his lips gently over hers and whispered, "It isn't enough to just hold you in my arms, Morgan. Now get out of this room—before we do something we'll both regret."

With his hands firmly on her shoulders, he turned her toward the door and gently shoved her away. In the doorway she hesitated and turned to look at him.

Kent had turned to stare at the flames licking the huge log in the fireplace. With his hand resting on the mantel, he seemed to be fighting for control. He held himself erect, almost as though he would soon give in to his desire to turn to her and call her back. In her aroused state, Morgan knew she could be easily persuaded to stay with him. And more than ever before, he seemed to want her.

With one last lingering look at his unyielding figure, Morgan turned and walked to her room without a word.

Chapter Nine

Morgan stood under the needle-sharp spray of the shower, feeling all of her senses tingling with a new awareness. She had spent the long, hollow hours before dawn reliving her scene with Kent. His tenderness and iron-willed control seemed further proof to her that he really cared for her.

Morgan smiled to herself. Despite the intrusion of Audrey Allen, it was going to be a beautiful day. Dressed in simple slacks and a cotton shirt, she brushed her still-damp hair loose and hurried to her office.

In the doorway she stopped short. Audrey, fully dressed, with hair and makeup complete, was seated in the wicker chair, reading Kent's manuscript.

Morgan struggled to keep her anger in check. In a carefully controlled voice, she asked, "Just what do you think you're doing, Miss Allen?" She kept her hands clenched tightly at her sides.

Audrey's head shot up, and she coldly regarded Morgan for a moment before dropping her head and continuing to scan the page.

In a bored voice, she commented, "Just what does it look like I'm doing? I'm reading my part."

"Your part!" Morgan couldn't believe what she had heard.

"Yes. My part. I intend to be given the lead in this movie. And I intend to see that it's the best part I've ever had. I've already told Kent I'll do anything to get this part. Anything!"

She waved a hand in Morgan's direction. "So, if you don't mind, I'd like to be left alone to see what Kent's written for me." In a petulant tone she added, "From what I've read so far, I'm not very impressed. My part isn't nearly as large as the male lead. When I get back home, I intend to phone Reynolds Standish and tell him exactly what I think of this screenplay."

At that, Morgan bristled defensively. This woman had no right to attack Kent's work. With her hands on her hips, she shot Audrey a murderous look. "You wouldn't do such a thing! From what I've read, Kent has written a marvelous screenplay. Why, if you complain to the director, you could ruin Kent's chances to become a screenwriter."

"Ruin Kent!" Audrey's voice whined sarcastically. She peered over the paper and stared at Morgan. "Why, you naïve little creature. Do you think I care that much?" With that she snapped her fingers.

"You make it sound like Kent Taylor is some poor, struggling . . ." The words froze on her lips as Kent loomed up behind Morgan.

"Audrey!" he bellowed.

Morgan whirled at the sound of his voice. Kent's eyes were blazing with fury. In one swift motion he crossed the room and snatched the manuscript from Audrey's hands. Towering over her, with his fists held close to his sides, he said in an ominously quiet tone, "I'd better get out of here before I forget you're a woman."

In the silence that followed, Audrey said coldly, "Yes, Kent. Maybe you had better get out of here . . ." and her voice whined in a near-perfect imitation of his smoldering order to Morgan just a few hours earlier by the light of the fire, ". . . before we do something we'll both regret."

Morgan's hand flew to her mouth to stifle a gasp. Audrey had witnessed their scene of the night before! How? Where? With a sinking heart Morgan realized that Audrey must have hidden herself in the darkened shadows and watched as she and Kent had nearly succumbed to the powerful feelings that had stirred in them.

Kent whirled and studied Audrey for a moment. His eyes blazed in fury. Morgan watched, helpless, as he fought to control his emotions. Suddenly a stiffness came over his face, changing his features into a rigid, unreadable mask.

With great effort, his hands still clenched, he said, "You would stoop to anything, wouldn't you, Audrey? You don't care what you do or whom you hurt, as long as you get what you want."

She returned his stare, and her mouth twisted into an evil leer. "That's right. And I've discovered an interesting little fact about you, too, darling. You've finally done it, haven't you, Kent? You think you've found true love," she said sarcastically.

He studied her for a long moment, then slowly turned away from her. Audrey reached out one perfectly manicured finger and jabbed at the flesh on his arm. He paused, his eyes narrow slits. In a voice husky with emotion, Audrey said, "Do you really think for a moment she can fit into your life?"

With deliberate care, Kent removed her finger from his arm and turned to her. Angrily, his words sliced the tension in the room. "That's enough, Audrey."

"No, darling. You will listen to me. I know what an idealist you are. Men like you—writers, dreamers —always believe there is a perfect woman somewhere in this great big world just waiting for a man like you." Her voice lowered conspiratorially. "If you think she's so perfect, so right for you, why won't you even trust her with the truth?"

Kent's fists tightened at his side. For a moment, Morgan thought he might strike Audrey. Then he slowly turned away. Morgan caught a glance at his face. It was bleak. Audrey's words had had the desired effect.

As he started across the room, Audrey called, "She'll betray you, Kent. You'll be sorry. I promise you."

Kent continued walking, and without even a glance in Morgan's direction, left the room. A moment later his bedroom door closed with a resounding slam that reverberated throughout the lodge.

The two women faced each other across the room.

Softly, Morgan said, "You are contemptible, Audrey!"

"And you are a foolish child, Morgan," Audrey said with venom. "Do you really believe a man like Kent can love someone like you?"

When Morgan refused to reply, Audrey continued, "I understand a man like Kent. He and I are alike," she said, smiling maliciously.

"Alike!" Morgan exclaimed, repelled by the thought.

"I know him much better than you, you little fool. We are both ambitious, driven to succeed." Her eyes raked over Morgan mercilessly. Contemptuously, she added, "Kent must be nearly twice your age. Why, you're nothing but a child, a toy for Kent to play with, to pass the time on this boring little island. A virile man like Kent will fill his needs with whatever happens to be available."

Drawing herself up to her full height, Audrey half-turned, displaying her voluptuous figure. With a sneer, she said, "You're a child, Morgan. You should stay in your room with the door locked."

Her remark was like a slap in the face to Morgan. Even the words Kent had murmured softly to her had been overheard by this hateful woman. Her face drained of all its color.

"A child, Morgan," Audrey repeated. "Trying to play adult games. Do you really think you can fit into Kent's world? Do you have any idea what kind of life he leads? His friends, his contemporaries, are sophisticated, wealthy, worldly people. A drab, un-sophisticated creature like you would be a—a mill-stone around Kent's neck."

As Morgan turned away, Audrey snapped, "Take a good look at yourself, Miss Mouse. What could a girl like you possibly offer a man like Kent Taylor?" With the polished poise of an actress, she brushed past Morgan and walked deliberately to her bed-room, leaving Morgan alone, still standing in the doorway.

Dazed, Morgan moved down the hall. So much of what Kent and Audrey had said to each other made no sense to her. Audrey's warning about a betrayal, for one thing. Morgan could never betray Kent. And what had she meant about the truth? What was the truth about Kent that he was afraid to reveal to Morgan?

In the kitchen, sunlight streamed through the windows. Morgan moved about the room, unable to shake her feeling of doom. She wasn't at all sure how she would react when she saw Kent again. When she had passed his room on her way to the kitchen, the door was still firmly closed.

She stared out the window at the blinding sunlight reflected off the water and frowned in concentration. All those hateful things Audrey had hurled at her were too close to the truth. She knew she was too naïve to understand a man like Kent. The seed of doubt that Audrey had planted was already begin-ning to grow in Morgan's mind, to torment her, to choke out any argument she might have to offer. How could she ever fight a woman like Audrey? And how could she hope to please a man like Kent? Why did she have to be so young—so inexperienced? She had no weapons with which to fight a woman like Audrey.

The kettle whistled. Morgan poured boiling water into a small teapot and frowned, still deep in thought. Audrey Allen expected to get the lead in the movie. In fact, she had made it plain that she would do anything for the part. Morgan slammed the kettle back on the stove. Anything! Audrey couldn't have made her intentions any clearer than that.

With her back to the door, she heard footsteps. Wiping her sweating palm on her shirt, Morgan forced herself to turn slowly. Kent was standing in the doorway, watching her.

"I've made some tea. Would you like some?" She felt relieved to notice that her voice hadn't betrayed her nervousness. She managed to sound almost normal.

"No," he said curtly. "I'll fix some coffee."

While he moved about the kitchen, Morgan sat at the table and watched him through lowered lashes. Kent slid into the chair across from her. Morgan racked her brain for trivial, unimportant things to talk about. Safe subjects. The weather. The scenery. Anything but the angry scene in her office.

"Have you ever been to your island in the winter?" she asked haltingly.

"Occasionally." His eyes were glazed, staring into space.

She thought for a moment he would refuse to say more. Finally, he added, "It's the perfect place when I need some solitude. This island is sealed off from civilization during the harshest part of the winter. Sometimes I need that isolation," he mused. Kent, too, seemed willing to talk of trivial things.

"Does your secretary come along?" Morgan asked.

"Helen?" Kent stared at her a moment, distracted, then looked away. "There's no way I could talk Helen into coming up here in the winter," he said. "She doesn't mind a month or so in the summer. But that's all the seclusion she can take. Besides, I don't need Helen for anything except the final typing. I prefer to work alone on the rough drafts of my work, then call on Helen for the later drafts. Helen is a native Californian," Kent explained. "She even complains if I want her to come to New York to work."

Morgan was pleased at the turn of the conversation. She wanted Kent to keep on talking about anything that wouldn't upset him.

"Do you have an office in New York?" she asked.

"No. I work out of an apartment there," he said, mentioning an address on Park Avenue.

Morgan knew the location and mentally concluded that he probably borrowed it from a wealthy friend.

"What do you do while you're in New York?" she asked, eager to keep him talking.

At his raised eyebrow, she added, "Do you have friends there? Writers? Artists? Someone you can talk to?"

"Some," he replied vaguely.

"How about in California?" she asked. "Do you know any celebrities?"

He stared across the table at her. Morgan knew she was babbling, but she so wanted to keep him talking about anything except Audrey and that terrible scene.

Very softly, he asked, "What is it you want to know, Morgan?"

She lowered her head, causing her hair to fall forward like a soft cloud about her cheeks. Kent's eyes studied her, lingering on her expressive, brown eyes. Instinctively, her lashes swept down defensively.

She wanted to know everything about him—what he was like as a child, his favorite food, what books he liked to read, his favorite color, whether he cared about her as much as she . . . loved him.

Blushing furiously, she replied, "Nothing special. I just wanted—to talk."

Tiredly, he asked, "Even knowing how much I dislike talking about myself?"

"But I need to know more about you," she persisted.

"Need to?" He watched her eyes.

"Yes," she said softly. "I want to know—you."

As she glanced up, the tender look in his eyes sent searing desire once again blazing through her veins. Her pulse raced.

He reached across the tabletop and caught her hand. She felt a jolt of pleasure at his touch.

"All right, Morgan," he said with resignation. "Ask me all your questions. I'm through fighting you. I'll tell you anything you want to know." In a monotone he added, "Maybe Audrey is right. I've been reluctant to—trust you."

Morgan's heartbeat quickened. Trust. It was a beginning.

In her excitement, the words tumbled out, one on top of another. "I want to know what you did here when you were a boy. And I want to know what you write when you're not writing screenplays. And tell me the famous people you've met in Hollywood. Like Reynolds Standish. He's such a famous . . ."

They both looked up, puzzled at the sound of the throbbing engines of Joe's launch.

Morgan and Kent hurried to the back porch and watched as the old man made his way carefully along the dock and up to the lodge.

"Hello, Joe," Kent called. "A fine day. What brings you here?"

"Mr. Taylor." He nodded toward Morgan, tipping his cap. "Miss. There's an important message from the States for you, Mr. Taylor. I hurried right over with it."

He handed an envelope to Kent, and both Joe and Morgan watched Kent's face as he tore open the envelope and read the paper inside.

"Morgan," Kent said abruptly, his face a grim mask. "If you'll fix Joe some coffee, I'll pack." Turning to Joe, he said, "I'll be just a few minutes. Can you wait and take me to the mainland?"

"What's happened, Kent?" Morgan asked in surprise.

"My mother is ill. I'll have to fly to Palm Springs immediately," he said, turning toward the door.

As he yanked open the door, he nearly collided with Audrey, who had overheard his comment.

"I'm going with you," she said.

"There's no need," Kent snapped.

"There certainly is. You don't think I'm going to stay in this dreary place without you. I'll be packed in a few minutes."

"You said Reynolds Standish was flying in his private plane for you at the end of the week," he said, eyeing her suspiciously.

"Well, I'll just phone him and explain that there's been a change of plans," she said through clenched teeth.

So, Morgan realized, that was why Kent had allowed Audrey to stay here. She had the director and his plane at her disposal. Audrey Allen had certainly made connections in high places. Hadn't she warned that she would do anything for the lead?

While Audrey and Kent hurried to their rooms, Morgan led Joe to the kitchen. She left him there a few minutes later seated at the table with a steaming cup of coffee.

At Kent's open door, she stopped. "Is there anything I can do to help?" she asked softly.

He looked up, and for a moment he only stared at her. Then he bent his head and continued packing.

Morgan stared at the fair hair spilling across his forehead as he packed hurriedly. She had an almost overpowering urge to brush back the lock with her hand. She felt a tiny shiver of pleasure as she recalled the feel of the silken strands as she had run comb and scissors through his hair.

Dropping a pile of clothing into his suitcase, Kent said, "I'll take the manuscript with me. I still have the final scenes to edit. I don't know if I'll manage to get any work done, but I can try."

"Should I get ready to leave, too?" Morgan asked.

"No!" he snapped. Checking his anger, he said more softly, "No, Morgan. Please. I'd like you to stay. Just until I know what I'm dealing with. If it's a minor problem, I may get back within a few days. Otherwise . . ." He interrupted his own thoughts: "Morgan, I'm leaving you with such a mess. There's so much unfinished business."

"I'll be all right here, Kent. I can manage."

"I'm sure you can," he said. "I think you can handle just about any situation."

He tilted her chin. Staring into her eyes, he asked softly, "You won't be afraid here all alone?"

In her heart she felt the cold blade of fear already beginning to slice at her confidence. But she forced herself to meet his steely gaze. "I don't know. Maybe. But I've been alone in strange situations before. I'll get by."

"Morgan, there's so much . . ." His thumb stroked her lips, and for a moment his look softened. He straightened suddenly and ran his hand roughly through his hair.

"Now listen," he said quickly. "I'll probably remember a million details later. For one thing, there's a time change between here and California. If you take the morning ferry to Port Elgin, you can reach me at this number." He bent and wrote on a slip of paper and handed it to her. "Tomorrow, at noon your time, I'll try to be there for your call. That's all we can plan for now."

"All right," she said. "Tomorrow, at noon, New Brunswick time. If I don't reach you, how will you reach me?" What a time to have no telephone, she thought miserably.

"I'll have to leave word for Joe. He can stop by with any messages."

She watched as he snapped his suitcase shut and lifted it off the bed. His eyes met hers. She couldn't read his look. She hoped her own eyes wouldn't betray her. She must not let him down. Or let him see what was in her heart.

He turned and walked briskly down the hallway toward the back porch. Morgan followed. Down at the dock Joe was already loading Audrey's luggage aboard the launch. Joe swung Kent's huge suitcase easily onto the deck.

Turning, Kent gave Morgan a tight smile.

"Good luck, Kent," she whispered.

"Thanks, Morgan," he murmured.

As he climbed aboard, Audrey reached out and clutched his arm. Smiling maliciously at Morgan, she called, "Goodbye, Miss Anders."

"Goodbye," Morgan said softly.

The boat eased from the dock and moved slowly to open water. Then, with a roar, it surged ahead. Audrey had settled in the corner of the boat. Kent stood alongside Joe at the wheel. He turned as they sped away and continued to stare at Hidden Island until they were out of sight.

Morgan stayed on the dock, hugging her arms about herself in the sudden chill she felt despite the brilliant sunlight. When the boat was finally just a dark spot on the horizon, she turned slowly and made her way to the lodge.

She had felt so elated this morning. So filled with hope. Now a feeling of foreboding hung over her like a pall. She couldn't shake off the feeling of pending doom.

Morgan stood in the phone booth outside the post office at Port Elgin and listened as the phone at the other end rang endlessly. Finally, just when she had decided there would be no answer, she heard the familiar deep voice.

"Hello," Kent said, sounding slightly out of breath.

"Kent. Hello." Suddenly, she forgot all the things she had planned to say. Her heart caught in her throat.

"Morgan. I was hoping you'd catch the ferry in time to phone me today. How is everything going?"

"Fine," she lied. She had just spent one of the worst nights of her life.

"I heard on the news this morning that there was a severe storm in New Brunswick. Did it hit the island?" he asked.

"Yes." Not only had the storm struck, but it had blown with such ferocity, that for a while Morgan had wondered if the lodge could withstand the fury.

"Was there any damage?" Kent asked.

"A little. Some tree branches down. The power is out. But a work crew assured me it would be restored by the time I get back there this afternoon."

Morgan didn't fill in the details. The power had

gone out at the height of the storm, leaving her groping about the lodge in the blackness until she located several candles in a kitchen cupboard. It had been a night of terror for her. But she had survived. And today, just hearing Kent's voice, everything seemed all right.

"Now," she said to change the subject, "tell me how your mother is."

"They're running tests at the hospital," he said. "It may be several more days before I even know what I'm dealing with here. The doctor says I have to be patient."

Morgan chuckled. Asking Kent Taylor to be patient was asking the impossible.

"The waiting must be an ordeal for her. And for you," Morgan said gently.

"Yes," he said distractedly. "But right now I'm more concerned about the fact that you were caught in that storm. I've seen what storms are like in New Brunswick. Morgan," Kent said emphatically, "if the power is still off on the island, you are not to stay there. Instead of going back on the ferry, have Joe take you back in the launch. That way, he can wait until you check out the lodge. If the power isn't on, have him take you back to Port Elgin. There's a little boardinghouse there. It's small and neat. I'm sure they'll put you up."

Morgan smiled at his commanding tone. "Yes sir," she said.

"I'm not joking, Morgan. I won't have you alone on that secluded island without any power. In fact, I don't like you being there alone at all. If I can't get back there within a few days . . ." He didn't finish the sentence.

Morgan sobered. "All right, Kent. I'll have Joe take me across and wait until I've checked out the lodge. Now, what is the weather like in Palm Springs?" she asked.

"Stifling. They practically close down this town in summer. It's probably one hundred and twenty degrees today. Not your ideal working conditions," he complained.

"Well, then, hurry back to Hidden Island. It couldn't be prettier. Now that the storm has passed," she said, laughing.

"Morgan . . ." His voice sounded gruff.

"Yes?"

"Take some time to see the countryside," he ordered.

"Yes. I will. Now, is there anything else?"

There was a moment of silence, and Morgan thought there might have been an interruption in their connection. Then, he said quietly, "No. Nothing else. Phone me the day after tomorrow. Noon, New Brunswick time. I'll be here."

"All right," she promised. "Goodbye, Kent."

"Goodbye, Morgan," he said gruffly.

Morgan replaced the receiver and stared for a moment at the telephone. It was her only link now with Kent. He seemed so far away. She shrugged and walked along the street toward the wharf. Skipping across puddles left by the night's storm, she suddenly began running. Morgan needed to see Hidden Island once again. To reassure herself that it

159

was real; that this whole summer had really happened; that Kent Taylor had actually lived there and met her and—touched her. All of a sudden, Morgan had the overpowering need to prove to herself that everything that had happened to her this summer hadn't just been some foolish, romantic dream.

Joe's launch was tied at the pier. His white head was bent over the engine, his gnarled hands gripping a wrench. He looked up as Morgan hopped aboard. Then his leathery face widened into a smile. His dark eyes showed a spark of humor.

"You are eager to go back to your island, eh, miss?"

"I wish it were my island, Joe," she said wistfully. "I'm in no hurry," she said patiently. "Whenever you're ready, so am I."

"I'll be just a few more minutes," he said, bending once more to his task. At last, Joe placed the wrench in a toolbox, closed the lid and wiped his hands on a rag. Standing, he said, "All finished. Now, miss, I take you to your island."

The waters of the strait were especially rough after the storm of the night before. Morgan gripped the edge of the rough, wooden seat and stared into the wind for a glimpse of the island. When it came into view, she smiled. It was a comforting sight.

"Home, miss," Joe said as he tied up the launch at the dock.

Morgan didn't bother to correct him. For the precious time that she had left here, this was her home. Her island.

While Morgan hurried to the lodge to see if the power was on, Joe walked along the shoreline, checking to see if any trees had been uprooted during the high winds. Morgan was relieved to find the lights back on. The huge generator had been restored by a crew from the mainland. Hurrying outside to relay the news to Joe, she came upon him hauling broken tree limbs to an open space.

"When this wood dries out, you can have a huge bonfire," he said, his face crinkling into a wide smile. "Judging by the size of some of these limbs, you must have had very strong winds during the height of the storm."

Morgan grimaced. "For a while I thought the lodge would blow away, with me in it."

"It is a good, solid lodge," he remarked, staring at the building. "It has seen worse storms than this one. And it survives, yet," he mused. "I will stop by each day to check on things until Mr. Taylor returns," he added softly.

Morgan felt a rush of gratitude for this gentle, old man. She watched as he walked slowly toward the dock. Then she turned and made her way to the lodge.

The following day Morgan caught the ferry to Prince Edward Island. The sky was a cloudless blue. The crowds of summer tourists were friendly and cheerful, and the tour guides were eager to show everyone a good time. Morgan should have been having the time of her life. She was finally getting a chance to see this lovely province. Yet she couldn't help missing Kent. All of this would have been such an adventure, if only she were doing it with him.

Tasting the delicacies prepared at quaint inns in colorful fishing villages, Morgan recalled the morning Kent had given her a brief history of the Acadian fishermen. That had meant more to her than a scenic cruise of their villages, which she could now see nestled in tiny coves and harbors. With Kent's sudden withdrawal from her life, everything seemed to have lost its flavor. Just one brief summer with him and nothing in her life was the same.

The next day, as arranged, Morgan met Joe at the dock and endured the rough, windy trek to the mainland. Standing in the phone booth, she felt the shock of hearing Kent's voice on the other end of the line. It was a painful reminder of the distance between them.

Through the static she said hesitantly, "Kent?"

There was no reply.

"Kent? What report have you had on your mother?"

"She's fine. It was nothing serious." His voice was strangely flat.

"Oh, I'm so glad. When will you be returning to Hidden Island?" Morgan was beaming with pleasure.

His staccato reply was a shocking assult. "I'm not coming back. There are a man and his wife on the mainland who always close up the lodge for the season. I'll send them out tomorrow. Pack your things. You can leave on tomorrow's ferry."

An awkward pause stretched out interminably. Finally, Morgan found her voice.

"Kent. Why?" She blinked back tears that were threatening to erupt.

"You know why, Morgan. No more games. Please," he said tiredly. "Your fun is over."

"Games? Fun? I don't understand what you're saying," she said, her voice trembling.

"Stop it, Morgan!" His voice cut through the phone line like a whip. "You've known all along, haven't you?"

"Known?" Her voice sounded too high, like a quivering child's voice.

"When you showed up on my doorstep. Pretending that you had innocently applied for the job without knowing who I was. You knew even then, didn't you, Morgan?" He paused, then continued without waiting for her protest. "And that 'friend' who conveniently worked for the New York *Press*. I had a hard time swallowing that lie. But I wanted so badly to believe you, Morgan."

In the phone booth Morgan leaned against the wall, unable to absorb what he was saying. His words continued lashing her, and she mutely held the phone.

"When you were so eager to find out all you could about me, I realized you could use every word I said in another of those twisted, vicious articles. But I wanted to think you were different from all those other reporters."

"Reporters?" She snapped to attention.

"And when I saw that first article in the New York *Press*, I knew it had to be written by you." He paused. "But then Audrey arrived on the island and said that Reynolds Standish had mentioned my 'velvet-voiced secretary' at a party, and I realized that a lot of people knew about you. So, once again I began to trust you. That article in the gossip column could have been told by anyone."

For the first time, Morgan began to realize what had sent Kent into a rage that afternoon in his room. He had spotted his name in a gossip column and had believed it was written by Morgan.

She held her breath, waiting for the next blow. When it came, it was swift and agonizing.

"But yesterday's article was too much, Morgan. After the New York *Press* came out with those lies, they were picked up by a national news magazine. How do you think I feel reading that pack of lies spread out on the cover of a magazine? 'Kensington T. Martin secluded on island of desire.' One article even went on to hint that after a summer with a girl young enough to be my daughter I flew into the waiting arms of actress Audrey Allen. The title of that bit of trash was 'Readers Need Scorecard.' It was the most twisted, vicious piece of junk I've ever read."

"Kensington T. Martin?" her voice rasped. "Kent, you're Kensington T. Martin?"

Morgan could hear his breath being expelled in fury.

"Stop the innocent act, Morgan!" he commanded.

Morgan stood in stunned silence as the reality of his words sank in. Kent Taylor was Kensington T. Martin, the famous writer. He believed that she had used her position here to spy on him. And he believed that she had written those horrible stories.

Her voice was strangled with pain and shock. "You can't really believe what you're saying!"

With a razor-sharp edge, he snapped, "Pack up and get out! I want you off the island by tomorrow. Helen will see to it that your final pay check is mailed to you in New York. Goodbye, Morgan. Your contract is terminated."

She heard the click and continued to hold the telephone in her sweating hand. Finally, she hung up the phone and leaned her forehead against the cool glass of the phone booth.

This wasn't really happening. It was crazy. All wrong. Kent—Kensington T. Martin. Not the struggling screenwriter she had thought him to be. She tried to think. Had he ever told her that himself? Her mind was a blur. No, she had just assumed that's what he was. And he had never bothered to correct her assumption. He let her go on this whole summer thinking he was some poor, struggling screenwriter. But in reality he was the very famous writer Kensington T. Martin. Playboy. Jet-setter. Womanizer. And he had the nerve to accuse her of ruining his reputation!

Morgan blinked back the tears stinging her eyelids and ran blindly to the wharf. For the first time she wasn't aware of the rough waves or the wind whipping her hair across her eyes. Wanly she thanked Joe for the ride and ran numbly toward the lodge. Birds chirped. Gulls cried. A distant speedboat droned across the waters of the strait. She saw and heard nothing. Kent wasn't coming back. Her summer adventure was ended.

Blinded by tears of humiliation, Morgan paced the floor of her room. Why had he deceived her like this? While she had spent the summer thinking she was helping some poor, unknown writer, he had been laughing at her secretly. Having his little joke at her expense. She stopped her pacing and moaned in anger. How foolish she had been! When she had spotted the name on that book she had brazenly defended his talent. She actually had told Kent that she thought Kensington T. Martin was a brilliant writer. And all this time Kent had been laughing at her. He had so many opportunities to tell her the truth about himself. But he had chosen to keep his secret. He hadn't deliberately lied to her. No. He had never come right out and said he was a poor, struggling screenwriter. She had come to that conclusion all by herself. But the shabby clothes, the unkempt appearance, the scraggly growth of hair . . .

And then a worse thought intruded. Kent was the infamous womanizer she had so often read about in the newspapers and magazines. No wonder he had become so enraged that night as he talked about reporters. He had been the object of countless gossip columns. And she had even allowed herself to think that Kent might be falling in love with her. Love! That—that man didn't know the meaning of the word. And with a nobody like her! No wonder Audrey had warned that she could never fit into Kent's world. Let him have Audrey Allen. They deserved each other, climbing over each other's fame to reach the top.

Without even the energy to pack, Morgan crawled into bed, finally giving in to the tears of anger and frustration that burned her eyes and throat.

The next morning, Morgan worked slowly as a feeling of lethargy gripped her mind and body. Listlessly, she moved through the rooms of the lodge, making certain that everything was in order. The couple Kent had hired from the mainland would arrive shortly on the ferry to see to it that shutters were set in place over the windows and that the lodge was securely steeled against the ravages of winter.

Standing just inside the doorway of her room, she allowed her eyes to scan the small space, imprinting in her mind all the details of the place where she had slept these quiet summer nights. The night table and dresser top were now bare of all clutter. Her bedding had been stripped and now lay neatly folded at the foot of the mattress. In the small bathroom all her toilet articles had been carefully packed. The room was bare, with no trace that she had ever been here. It was as though a painting of the entire summer had been erased with a single stroke of the artist's brush.

In the kitchen Morgan washed the last of her dishes and put them away in the cupboard. Her eyes fastened on the yellow daisy cup and saucer that Kent had bought in town on their special day. Sadly, she closed the cupboard door, as though trying to blot out the memory of that happy time. On the back porch, she hung the towel to dry, then walked slowly through the lodge, allowing her mind to absorb all the familiar rooms, now cold and barren, as though asleep until the next time they came alive for their owner. For the first time since her arrival on this tiny island, Morgan felt the alien prickle of loneliness.

She made her way outdoors for one last, lingering tour of the island. Her eyes trailed over the tall growth of Queen Anne's lace, yellow daisies and wild roses. Would Kent be reminded of her the next time he came here? She sighed. By then he probably would have forgotten her name.

At the water's edge she turned to take in the sight of the lodge. It was such a sturdy building, braving the winds of winters past. With a bittersweet sadness, she realized that this had been the home of Kent in his earlier, innocent boyhood.

Oh, why had she come here? This had started out to be a carefree summer job. A lark. A chance to get away from the teeming city for a while and earn the extra money she needed. But it had gone wrong from the very beginning. When her car broke down on that stormy night, she should have seen it as an omen of things to come.

Kent Taylor, she thought bitterly. Everything about the man was a sham. Even his name. Liar, cheat, fraud! He had hurled those hateful words at her that first awful night. But he was the liar, the cheat, the fraud!

Morgan turned from the shore. The frothy waves erased her footprints as she moved away. Making her way toward the porch, where her suitcase and overnight bag stood packed and ready for the journey home, she stared around the island. Almost from the beginning, this place had had a mystical, otherworldly quality about it. Maybe it was just because it was so isolated from the world, or maybe because it had seemed like a tiny, imaginary kingdom, with Kent Taylor its king. Hadn't she sometimes felt that they were completely shut away from the rest of the world? Each day, as she had awakened, there had been a sense of expectancy. As though something wonderful would happen.

As the foghorn blasted from the ferry, Morgan scooped up her baggage and made her way to the dock. A man of about fifty was helping his wife down the ramp. They both smiled as Morgan approached.

"Miss Anders?" the man asked.

Morgan smiled and offered her hand.

"My wife and I are here to close up the Taylor lodge for the season. We've taken care of it before," he assured her.

The woman nodded and smiled. "Don't worry about a thing, dear. We've done all this before. You have a good trip, now."

"Thank you. Goodbye." Morgan picked up her luggage and boarded the ferry, going to the rail for one last glimpse of Hidden Island.

All morning long, she realized now, she had been secretly nurturing the tiny, flickering hope that Kent would come striding back to his island and make everything all right. What a foolish dreamer she was. She angrily chided herself for her silly fantasy. Those things only happened in movies. This was reality. Kent was a thousand miles away, involved in his own life. By now she had been completely erased from his thoughts.

As the island receded in the distance, Morgan felt the hot sting of tears—the tears that had been threatening to spill over all morning. In a gesture of angry defiance, Morgan brushed them away with the back of her hand. Kent Taylor wasn't worth her tears. But, she realized sadly, he had given her fair warning. She could still see him facing her across the table at the diner in Port Elgin that first morning, daring her to go back to that lonely strip of land with him. And she had naïvely taken up the challenge. And lost.

Morgan sighed. In her mind she would always be able to see the tall, athletic figure moving with the sleek, graceful stride of a lion, the wild mane of blond hair that spilled across a wide, thoughtful forehead, the strange tawny eyes, gold-flecked in the sunlight, now narrowed in concentration, now blazing in controlled anger. Eyes that were hazel in the firelight, sometimes gray, then again colorless. She had once wondered if the image would dim in time. Morgan stared down at the foam churning from the propellers far below. His image was so deeply imprinted in her memory that the thought of his touch made her tremble. The image of Kent Taylor was burned into her very soul.

When the ferry docked at Port Elgin, Morgan strained under the weight of her luggage. At the gas station she waited while Alphonse Gagnon finished filling a customer's tank.

"I'm leaving today, Mr. Gagnon," she said with as much cheer as she could muster. "I came for my car."

"I'll get your key," he said.

After she loaded her luggage in her battered old car, Alphonse Gagnon allowed a slow smile. He admired this spunky young woman.

"The best of luck to you, Miss Anders. You drive carefully, now," he said.

She reached through the open car window and

shook his hand. "Thanks for everything, Mr. Gagnon. And good luck to you, too."

She switched on the ignition. It caught and purred smoothly. She drove slowly away. In the rearview mirror, the image of the Northumberland Strait and the distant, tiny, green island faded into a blur.

Chapter Ten

A bleak, autumn wind whipped along the sidewalk, sending a fine spray of grit chafing at Morgan's red cheeks. A tiny whirlwind picked up debris from a gutter, spiraling it upward toward the second story of the apartment building. Crowds of people hurried by, eager to reach their destinations. Somewhere down the block a siren screamed. With head bent against the cold, Morgan hurried up the steps and leaned into the heavy outer door of her apartment building. Inside, a sudden blast of warmth greeted her.

With her new compact car in repair, Morgan was again forced to walk several blocks from the bus stop. On top of that, the city was in the grip of a cold snap. For the past three days the temperature had reached new lows, with a record-breaking early snowfall to add to the trouble.

She climbed two sets of stairs and set down her shopping bag to fish in her purse for her door key. Stepping into her apartment, she kicked the door shut behind her and hurried to the kitchen with her groceries.

An hour later, wrapped in a warm, fleece robe, her hair wet from the steaming shower, she sat in a comfortable chair in the living room, cradling a cup of soup in her hands. The television set provided a pleasant diversion. In the middle of the news broadcast her eyes widened in surprise. There on the screen was Audrey and a handsome actor, shown gyrating on a crowded dance floor in a club here in New York.

As the news broadcast moved on to other events, Morgan angrily snapped off the set and sank back down in the chair. Now it would start again; all the memories would flood back to torment her. Each time she thought she was getting over Kent and that dreamlike summer, something happened to bring it all back into painfully sharp focus.

Since she had returned to New York, there had been no word from Kent. Her final paycheck had arrived, signed in an unfamiliar hand. His secretary, Helen, was back taking care of his business. There had been no correspondence, and she had read very little about Kent since her return.

Her resumption of her normal life had been accomplished with surprising speed. Within weeks she was once again working at the office of Fairfield Academy. The staff members were too busy getting back to the routine in their classrooms to spend much time discussing their summer jobs. When the question did come up, Morgan simply said she had taken a job in Canada for the summer. There was no reason to go into detail.

Morgan picked up her dishes and walked to the tiny kitchen of her apartment. As happened so often, she found herself recalling all the details of her summer with Kent. Pausing, she reminded herself with a shrug that he was not worth all the pain she had suffered. But even the knowledge of his unforgivable attack on her character didn't ease the hurt. It only made it worse. Even though she constantly had reminded herself that any man who could believe that she was capable of such deceit didn't deserve her love, she wasn't able to eliminate Kent from her thoughts.

She needed only to close her eyes, and she could recall in sharp detail everything about Kent: the fine strands of corn-silk hair spilling across his forehead, the lean strength of his body, the warmth of his touch, the tawny eyes reflecting his moods. But most of all, she could recall the shocking tremors she had experienced at his kiss. No one had ever made her feel that way before. Perhaps no one else ever could again. The overpowering feelings she had experienced with Kent had spoiled her for any other man. How could anyone measure up to Kent?

After her return to New York, an enterprising reporter from a news magazine had approached her with a suggested story about Kent. She adamantly had refused an interview. The money offered was tempting. Even more tempting was the certain knowledge that an article revealing her summer employment would infuriate Kent, no matter how he might pretend to be used to such exploitation. How she would have loved to even the score with him! But she couldn't bring herself to do it. In the end, her sense of fair play won out over her sense of outrage.

The same couldn't be said of Audrey Allen, who apparently was not above using any publicity stunt to further her career. Just a few weeks after her return to New York, Morgan had read an account in a scandal sheet, supposedly told by Audrey Allen, of a romantic trip through New Brunswick with the famous author Kensington T. Martin. Morgan frowned every time she thought about the article. The story had made it sound as though Audrey and Kent had spent the entire summer together touring Canada. In the interview Audrey insisted that she had only admitted the truth because of earlier, misleading stories. Morgan wasn't convinced. In fact, she felt certain that it had to be Audrey who had orchestrated the entire scandal in order to gain the necessary publicity to win the coveted part in the Reynolds Standish movie.

After weeks of keeping her emotions carefully in check, refusing to allow herself to even think about Kent or her summer at the island, the article in the paper had brought a flood of memories rushing back. Morgan had lain awake that night, allowing herself to dwell on every word he had spoken in tenderness, every touch, every kiss. And for days afterward, she had found herself irritated at simple frustrations. She had even become snappish with friends at work. It had required all the discipline she could manage to force herself to stop reliving the past.

Morgan paused at the sink. Kent had told her that he was accustomed to the kind of publicity generated by magazine articles like the one Audrey had penned. After reading Audrey's nauseating, fictionalized account of a summer romance, Morgan at least understood just why Kent had been so cynical. And it had taught her not to believe all the things about celebrities she read in those columns.

Now, seeing Audrey on the news, Morgan realized with a sinking heart that it would all begin again. All the painful memories would return to haunt her. Her sleep would be disturbed; her nerves would grow taut. It would take her weeks to calm down.

That man! That infuriating man! Why did he ever come into her life! Wadding the kitchen towel into a ball, she angrily tossed it against the wastebasket, knocking it over and spilling the contents all over the floor. With an angry moan, she stooped to clean up the mess. So much for temper tantrums, she thought wryly.

The loud knock on the door startled her. Her upstairs neighbor often stopped over if her salesman-husband was out of town.

Morgan dried her hands on a towel and hung it on a hook. Flinging the door open, she muttered, "I'm sorry, Annie, but I'm not in the mood to . . ."

Her eyes widened in shock, then narrowed to tiny

slits of anger. "You!" she gasped at the sight of Kent filling the doorway.

As she moved to close the door on him, his hand stopped her.

She faced him, feeling her heart pounding painfully in her throat. "Get out of my apartment," she ordered him.

"Suit yourself," he said blandly. "But your neighbors will hear me shouting through the door."

"You wouldn't dare."

"Try me," he threatened.

Morgan knew, by the arrogant stance, by the strange light in those dusky eyes, that he meant what he said. She didn't want her neighbors peering suspiciously through their doors. Dropping her hand, she moved back a pace. Kent closed the door and faced her. Standing so near him, she felt the blood drumming in her temples. She moved to the far side of the room and stood, her arms crossed about her chest defensively.

"How did you find my apartment?" she asked.

"That was easy. Your address is in my file. Remember?"

His eyes carefully studied her, noting the thin, almost frail, figure. Her high cheekbones seemed even more prominent.

"You've lost weight," he said abruptly.

"Have I? I hadn't noticed," she said indifferently.

"How have you been, Morgan," he asked, suddenly changing moods.

"I've been just fine. Terrific," she said sarcastically. "And you?"

"Fine. Just fine. Couldn't be better." He nodded toward the chair. "Mind if I sit down?"

"Yes," she snapped. "I do mind. Say whatever you came here to say, and leave."

"How do you know I came here to say anything?" he asked.

"Because you didn't take the time to find me just to reminisce about old times." Morgan felt close to tears. How could he calmly walk back into her life and expect her to behave civilly? And why did he have to look so tall and cool and in control? The torment of being in the same room with him and not being able to touch him was tearing her apart.

"They spelled your name wrong," he commented mildly.

"They who? I don't know what you're talking about," she said angrily.

"In that article in the New York *Press*. The one that got picked up by the national news magazines. They spelled your name wrong." He studied her. "Didn't you notice?"

"Of course not. I never read it," she said in disgust.

"Really?" He raised one eyebrow quizzically. "Most publicity-seekers make certain the reporters spell their names right."

Morgan could feel her temper rising. This man, with his smug, superior attitude, had come here to bait her.

"Is that all you came here to say?" she asked. "If so, you've said it. Now leave."

"I'm afraid I can't leave just yet," Kent said, suddenly serious.

"You have no choice, Kent. I'm ordering you to leave," she said, striding across the room.

Before she could reach the door, his hand caught her arm. Morgan froze, feeling sudden shock waves colliding in her brain. His mere touch was enough to set her on fire. Recoiling from his touch, she shrank back against the wall. Kent towered over her, daring her to meet his gaze.

"Why did you come here, Kent?" she whispered.

His features were cold, unreadable. "I have a problem, Morgan," he said. "I keep remembering someone who spent last summer with me on an island. She keeps flitting in and out of my mind. And she seems so innocent. Too good, almost, to be true." He moved a step nearer, towering above her. "I've always prided myself on being able to spot a phony." His finger trailed around the curve of her cheek, sending tiny, icy shivers along her spine. With one deft movement, he curled his finger beneath her chin and lifted her face for his inspection. "So why do I keep having all these conflicting feelings for her?" he asked suddenly.

Morgan stepped aside, breaking contact with him. She couldn't bear his touch. Her throat was constricted, making breathing painful.

As she tore her gaze from him, he added, "Audrey said you were an ambitious, scheming amateur out to make a name for yourself."

"And of course, you choose to believe Audrey," she snapped.

Morgan felt crushed at the thought of Kent believing that evil woman. With a sinking heart, she realized that she had hoped, just for a few moments, that Kent had come here to declare his love for her. Love! Audrey was right. Kent and Audrey were alike. Both ambitious, clawing their ways to the top. And she had just been a toy for Kent to pass the long summer months on a lonely island.

"Believe what you want!" she flared.

"I wanted to believe in you," he said softly.

Morgan whirled to study him, but already the mask was slipping back into place, hardening his features. The dark, perfectly tailored suit over a pale silk shirt gave him an elegant, aloof appearance. The gruff, intense, tousled, careless Kent Taylor had been replaced by the successful author Kensington T. Martin.

"I think you'd better go now, Kent," she said sharply.

"Yes. You're right. But I would like to ask you one question, Morgan." His eyes glittered dangerously.

"What is it?" she asked, suddenly alert.

"Were you the one who reported that story?" He was watching her closely.

His question sliced through her like a razor. With great effort, she sought to control her trembling hands. Why had he waited so long to ask her? Why hadn't he asked her this question that day on the telephone, instead of accusing her so savagely?

Her hands were clenched so tightly at her sides, the knuckles were white from the effort. She stood rigidly facing him, her eyes blazing, her chin jutting defiantly.

With icy calm, she said through gritted teeth, "I will not dignify that disgusting question with a reply." She watched his features grow dark and angry. "You made up your mind a long time ago, Kent. You listened to Audrey on the flight home to Palm Springs. I'm sure she managed to plant quite a few seeds of doubt in your mind. It didn't take much more to convince you. And now, you're here making some sort of gesture. I don't pretend to understand just why you came. But it's all too little, too late." Tiredly, she added, "Just get out of my life. Now."

He turned stiffly away and headed toward the door. In a haze of pain, Morgan watched as he walked through the doorway and out of the room. She knew with startling clarity that she would never see him again. Kent was walking out of her life for good. After the way he had hurt her, she should feel relieved. Instead, she felt a numbing pain.

She turned, gripping the back of the chair. Good riddance! How dare he accuse her of such deceit! How dare he doubt her sincerity! If he really loved her, he would have known that she wasn't capable of such treachery.

With her hand clutched against her mouth, a new thought crashed through her mind with blinding pain. Wasn't she guilty of the same crime? Hadn't she allowed Audrey's insinuations to poison her against Kent? Hadn't she believed the lies Audrey had told her, convinced that Kent couldn't possibly love someone as naïve as she? Hadn't she fallen into the same trap as Kent? Didn't she still think him capable of all those things he was accused of in those many vicious gossip columns, even though she knew they were probably as false as Audrey's story had been?

If he didn't care about her, why had he swallowed his pride and come here tonight?

With a gasp, Morgan bolted through the opened doorway and flew down the two flights of stairs. Outside, Kent was just stepping into a chauffeur-driven limousine.

"*Kent! Wait!*" she shouted.

He whirled and watched her as she ran, barefoot, across the sidewalk. The blast of frigid air against her skin jolted her. Angrily, he caught her arm and roughly hurled her into the plush interior of the limousine.

"You little fool!" he hissed through clenched teeth. "It's freezing out here."

As he pulled shut the door, all the street sounds were instantly closed out. With the flick of a button, the glass partition silently glided up, sealing off their words from the uniformed driver.

He sat facing her, a frown of suspicion darkening his features.

"Now what, Morgan?" he demanded impatiently.

"Ask me again, Kent," she whispered.

"Ask you what?" he said, his eyes stormy gray with anger.

"Ask me your question again," she insisted.

He studied her for a long, agonizing minute before asking, "Were you the one who reported that story?"

The silence between them was charged with an electric current. Crystal tears glittered in Morgan's wide eyes.

In a quivering voice, she sighed, "Oh, Kent. If only you had asked me that in the first place, instead of accusing me so viciously on the telephone, you would have known that I couldn't betray you. How could I, when I love you so?"

His eyebrows drew together in a puzzled frown.

She rushed on. "I'm not sure how long I've loved you. I guess for most of the summer. And when I first left Hidden Island, I thought my heart would never stop aching. But I managed finally to convince myself that I hated you for accusing me, for not believing in me, for allowing Audrey Allen to plant the seeds of doubt and suspicion in your mind. I really thought that you couldn't possibly believe all those horrible things about me if you cared for me."

Kent continued to stare at her, saying nothing.

"Kent, when you walked out that door just now, I felt as though my world had ended. And I realized that even though I love you more than I've ever loved anyone in my whole life, I doubted you, too. I allowed Audrey to poison my thoughts against you. And if I can love you this much, and still doubt you, then maybe you love me, too, even though you have doubts about me."

She stared into his eyes, begging him to see the truth of her words. With great control, he held her stiffly at arm's length, staring at her silently.

Suddenly, with a rasping sob, the tears that had been threatening spilled over, ran down her cheeks. She turned her head, unable to bear the look in his eyes any longer. "What a fool I've been!" she sobbed. "I thought, just for a minute, that you had come back to discover the truth because you loved me as much as I love you. I should have known! You just came back for revenge. To torment me!"

183

"Stop it, Morgan!" he said savagely.

Her face came up as though she had been slapped. She watched as he struggled to control his emotions. Suddenly the mask of control slipped, and a look of pain crossed his face. Green points of flame danced in his tawny eyes.

"I do love you, Morgan," he whispered as he drew her into his arms.

As his mouth descended upon hers, she offered her lips hungrily. Tiny splinters of desire burst through her veins.

"And you do believe me?" she asked against his lips.

"And I do believe you," he murmured, nibbling her lips and pulling her roughly against him.

"Oh, Kent," she sighed against his throat. "Why did you wait so long?"

"Because I'm pig-headed," he murmured with his lips against her temple. "I didn't want to admit that a slip of a girl like you could cause me so much torment."

She felt the warmth of laughter in his voice as he brought his mouth against hers.

When their kiss ended, Morgan said, "Audrey said I'd never fit into your world."

Angrily he growled, "I never want to hear her name mentioned again." Drawing her closer into the circle of his arms, he whispered, "I need you in my world, Morgan. It's such an empty life without you."

He chuckled again, drawing her tightly to him. "When I first saw you standing on the front porch, looking like a drowned kitten . . ." Kent ran a hand through his hair and went on, ". . . and then in my robe, scared, so tired you were ready to drop, but still willing to stand up to me, ready to fight me. I guess I began to love you even then." He pressed his lips to the top of her head. "Ever since you came into my life, I've been watching all my control slip."

As she looked up at him in disbelief, Kent said, "I've never met anyone like you. When I realized just how much you were beginning to mean to me, I had to work overtime to keep my distance. I wouldn't have done anything to hurt you, but I knew it was only a matter of time before I would let down my guard and let you know my feelings for you. Morgan," he said, shaking his head in wonder, "I've never met anyone as self-assured as you."

"Self-assured," she said in surprise. "Kent, if you only knew what meeting you did to my confidence." She sighed. "By the time I finally realized just how much you meant to me, I thought I had lost you forever."

"Forever," he murmured, drawing her against his chest. "That's a beautiful word. Morgan, will you be my wife forever? I want you to be my wife, my lover, my friend, my companion, my . . ."

"Your cook," she laughed. "You definitely need a cook."

"Definitely. A cook," he said, nibbling her ear. "But most of all, Morgan, I just want to spend the rest of my life loving you."

"Oh, Kent," she said breathlessly, snuggling into his arms. "I can't think of anything I want more."

"And you don't mind that I'm that writer with the terrible reputation?" he asked.

She heard the warm laughter in his voice. "Kent, I don't care about your talent, your success, or your reputation. I love *you,* the person I knew last summer."

"I've waited a lifetime to hear someone say that," he murmured. "Morgan, my love, everything I have is yours." His lips traced a lazy pattern down her throat, burning her flesh. "And where we spend our time together is your choice. There's a chalet in Switzerland, an apartment outside Paris, plus the house in California and the apartment here in New York. Where would you like to spend your honeymoon?" He lifted his head, his eyes glinting with humor. "Not that you will get to see much of the countryside. I have other plans besides sightseeing."

"Oh, Kent," she breathed against his lips. "I do love you so."

As their kiss deepened, Morgan felt her heartbeat quicken. They would have forever to discover all the secrets of each other. There would be time enough later, a lifetime in fact, to explore the fascinating world in which Kent lived and worked. The world Morgan would share.

But for now she was determined that they would begin their new life together where it had started. On a tiny, secluded island inhabited only by two people who had waited a long time to express their love.

IT'S YOUR OWN SPECIAL TIME

Contemporary romances for today's women.
Each month, six very special love stories will be yours
from SILHOUETTE. Look for them wherever books are sold
or order now from the coupon below.

$1.50 each

☐ 5 Goforth	☐ 28 Hampson	☐ 54 Beckman	☐ 83 Halston
☐ 6 Stanford	☐ 29 Wildman	☐ 55 LaDame	☐ 84 Vitek
☐ 7 Lewis	☐ 30 Dixon	☐ 56 Trent	☐ 85 John
☐ 8 Beckman	☐ 32 Michaels	☐ 57 John	☐ 86 Adams
☐ 9 Wilson	☐ 33 Vitek	☐ 58 Stanford	☐ 87 Michaels
☐ 10 Caine	☐ 34 John	☐ 59 Vernon	☐ 88 Stanford
☐ 11 Vernon	☐ 35 Stanford	☐ 60 Hill	☐ 89 James
☐ 17 John	☐ 38 Browning	☐ 61 Michaels	☐ 90 Major
☐ 19 Thornton	☐ 39 Sinclair	☐ 62 Halston	☐ 92 McKay
☐ 20 Fulford	☐ 46 Stanford	☐ 63 Brent	☐ 93 Browning
☐ 22 Stephens	☐ 47 Vitek	☐ 71 Ripy	☐ 94 Hampson
☐ 23 Edwards	☐ 48 Wildman	☐ 73 Browning	☐ 95 Wisdom
☐ 24 Healy	☐ 49 Wisdom	☐ 76 Hardy	☐ 96 Beckman
☐ 25 Stanford	☐ 50 Scott	☐ 78 Oliver	☐ 97 Clay
☐ 26 Hastings	☐ 52 Hampson	☐ 81 Roberts	☐ 98 St. George
☐ 27 Hampson	☐ 53 Browning	☐ 82 Dailey	☐ 99 Camp

$1.75 each

☐ 100 Stanford	☐ 110 Trent	☐ 120 Carroll	☐ 130 Hardy
☐ 101 Hardy	☐ 111 South	☐ 121 Langan	☐ 131 Stanford
☐ 102 Hastings	☐ 112 Stanford	☐ 122 Scofield	☐ 132 Wisdom
☐ 103 Cork	☐ 113 Browning	☐ 123 Sinclair	☐ 133 Rowe
☐ 104 Vitek	☐ 114 Michaels	☐ 124 Beckman	☐ 134 Charles
☐ 105 Eden	☐ 115 John	☐ 125 Bright	☐ 135 Logan
☐ 106 Dailey	☐ 116 Lindley	☐ 126 St. George	☐ 136 Hampson
☐ 107 Bright	☐ 117 Scott	☐ 127 Roberts	☐ 137 Hunter
☐ 108 Hampson	☐ 118 Dailey	☐ 128 Hampson	☐ 138 Wilson
☐ 109 Vernon	☐ 119 Hampson	☐ 129 Converse	☐ 139 Vitek

Genuine Silhouette sterling silver bookmark for only $15.95!

What a beautiful way to hold your place in your current romance! This genuine sterling silver bookmark, with the distinctive Silhouette symbol in elegant black, measures 1½" long and 1" wide. It makes a beautiful gift for yourself, and for every romantic you know! And, at only $15.95 each, including all postage and handling charges, you'll want to order several now, while supplies last.

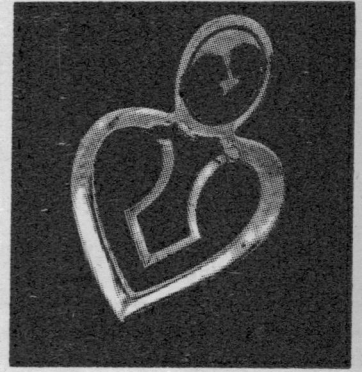

Send your name and address with check or money order for $15.95 per bookmark ordered to
Simon & Schuster Enterprises
120 Brighton Rd., P.O. Box 5020
Clifton, N.J. 07012
Attn: Bookmark

Bookmarks can be ordered pre-paid only. No charges will be accepted. Please allow 4-6 weeks for delivery.

N.Y. State Residents
Please Add Sales Tax

15-Day Free Trial Offer
6 Silhouette Romances

6 Silhouette Romances, free for 15 days! We'll send you 6 new Silhouette Romances to keep for 15 days, absolutely free! If you decide not to keep them, send them back to us. You pay nothing.

Free Home Delivery. But if you enjoy them as much as we think you will, keep them by paying the invoice enclosed with your free trial shipment. We'll pay all shipping and handling charges. You get the convenience of Home Delivery and we pay the postage and handling charge each month.

Don't miss a copy. The Silhouette Book Club is the way to make sure you'll be able to receive every new romance we publish before they're sold out. There is no minimum number of books to buy and you can cancel at any time.

This offer expires November 30, 1983

Silhouette Book Club, Dept. **SRSR7A**
120 Brighton Road, Clifton, NJ 07012

Please send me 6 Silhouette Romances to keep for 15 days, absolutely free. I understand I am not obligated to join the Silhouette Book Club unless I decide to keep them.

NAME_____

ADDRESS_____

CITY_____STATE_____ZIP_____

Get the Silhouette Books Newsletter every month for a year.

Now you can receive the fascinating and informative Silhouette Books Newsletter 12 times a year. Every issue is packed with inside information about your favorite Silhouette authors, upcoming books, and a variety of entertaining features—including the authors' favorite romantic recipes, quizzes on plots and characters, and articles about the locales featured in Silhouette books. Plus contests where you can win terrific prizes.

The Silhouette Books Newsletter has been available only to Silhouette Home Subscribers. Now you, too, can enjoy the Newsletter all year long for just $19.95. Enter your subscription now, so you won't miss a single exciting issue.

Silhouette Books